AIRSHIP 27 PRODUCTIONS

Sinbad-The New Voyages Volume Two

SINBAD & THE SWORD OF SOLOMON © 2013 Edward M. Erdelac
A DETOUR FOR SINBAD © 2013 Erwin K. Roberts
SINBAD & THE GOLDEN MASK © 2013 Shelby Vick

Published by Airship 27 Productions
www.airship27.com
www.airship27hangar.com

Interior illustrations © 2013 Steve Wilcox
Cover illustration © 2013 Kevin A. Johnson

Editor: Ron Fortier
Associate Editor: Charles Saunders
Production and design: Rob Davis
Marketing and Promotions: Michael Vance

ISBN-13: 978-0615861500
ISBN-10: 0615861504

Printed in the United States of America

10 9 8 7 6 5 4 3 2 1

SINBAD
the New Voyages
Volume Two
TABLE of CONTENTS

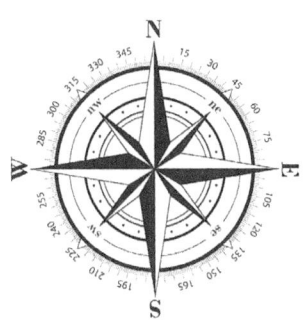

Sinbad & The Sword of Solomon

By Edward M. Erdelac

The Baghdad marketplace at noon clamored with a roar that surpassed most battles, with sellers fighting to thrust their wares past grim palanquin bearers at their wealthy, silk swaddled charges, like a phalanx of spearmen seeking a guarded commander. Haggling buyers besieged the stalls and shouted at the harried vendors in tones an untrained ear would think were cries of war. Livestock chattered, flapped, and bellowed as someone led a trained bear down the street, and a thousand curses upon that fool's head ascended to the ear of Allah like the pleas of men endangering their own lives for shah or chieftain.

But the closest thing to a real skirmish was underway in a quieter part of the market, in the dim shop of the venerable master sword maker Abdul al-Roozbeh, where Sinbad the sailor and the unlikely crew of the Blue Nymph had turned from the gleaming yatahgans and silver chased scimitars on display in endless variety to argue among themselves over whose culture had produced the greatest blade.

"Is it not said that 'there is no hero but Ali and no sword but Zulfiqar?'" said Omar, the stout, gray bearded Sindhi and iron hearted first mate of the Blue Nymph.

"Blasphemer," chuckled Sinbad, a bright, roguish smile flashing across his darkly handsome face as he idly smoothed his down swept mustache and shook his blue turbaned head.

"What blasphemy, Captain?" Omar said, throwing open his rough hands. "Was not Zulfiqar given unto Ali by the Prophet himself, bless his name? And did it not cleave the giant Amr ibn Abdawud, whose strength was like a thousand men, in twain and his armor and his shield?"

"It is blasphemy indeed to think a little Arab pigsticker could claim such a distinction," rumbled the bearded young blue eyed giant, Ralf Gunarson, in his badly accented Arabic. "Your brittle little blades are fit only for table eating, and for cleaning the dung out from between a camel's toes."

The great golden haired youth said these things in a spirit of jest or Omar should never have tolerated it. The two bickered endlessly as com-

5

rades. Also, it could be noted, the north man spoke out of ear shot of old Abdul al-Roozbeh, who had retired through a beaded curtain to the backroom upon the start of the conversation.

"So speaks the overgrown infant. Go out in the market, o master of calamities," growled Omar. "I believe I saw one of your barbarous kin being led on a leash, causing a ruckus among the poultry. What do you know of swords? A north man's idea of a weapon is what a Persian uses to chop wood."

"Aye, and this axe has felled forests pink and brown, little man," Ralf said, patting the haft of the ten pound battleaxe on his back. "But if we are speaking of swords forged by the gods, surely there could be no greater weapon than Gram, the sword of wrath, cast and hammered by Wayland, which Odin himself drove into the Barnstokk tree...."

"You see?" Omar scoffed, nudging Sinbad. "Tree."

"....and could cleave an anvil in two," Ralf finished, scowling at the grey bearded sailor with a look that said he might loose his great axe in the next moment.

"In my land," said Henri, the quick little archer from Gaul, "I once heard tell of a legendary blade."

"Ah yes, now we will hear from the Christian," Omar said, rolling his eyes. "And an archer too. Who better to speak on a sword? Let us call the melon seller in and ask his opinion next."

"Go on, Henri," Sinbad urged, when Omar had run out of breath.

"It was called Durendal, and its golden hilt was said to carry relics of St. Peter, and a scrap of the Virgin Mary's garment. The hero Roland supposedly held off ten thousand Saracens in the Pyrenees with it, to cover the retreat of the emperor Charlemagne, and when he saw that he would fall, he cast it into the cliff face and broke a mountain down."

"Supposedly," Omar said, folding his thick arms. "And let us suppose that a Frank could hold off ten thousand Muslims with anything other than his odor."

Henri laughed appreciatively behind his prodigious mustache, and Sinbad and Ralf joined in.

"You Christians. You call every man an infidel and yet even this great pagan from the north puts no special reverence in old toenails or women's clothing," Omar went on.

"Surely not a virgin's anyway," Ralf agreed, chuckling.

Omar turned to see the girl Tishimi watching him, inscrutable as ever.

"Yes? And what does our good luck charm have to say on the matter?"

They all turned to regard her. Though a comely woman, and slight, her foreign appearance and mode of dress caused most in Baghdad to mistake her for a youthful boy. She would never have been allowed into the master's shop uncovered otherwise, though she had proven herself time and time again to be the best sword fighter of them all, save perhaps for Sinbad.

"My father always said that even the greatest sword is as nothing if the hand that wields it is commanded by a fool," she said quietly.

Sinbad grinned his approval and the laughter of the old master smith rippled from the back room.

"Well said, young master. Well said."

The old man came from behind the beaded curtain, bearing a long, ornamented teakwood case, which he laid upon the counter and unlocked with an iron key from around a chain on his neck beneath his robes.

He turned the case as Sinbad and his mates gathered closer, and opened it.

What lay within was a sword that put to shame any they had seen with their own eyes. Bejewelled, yes, the golden hilt encircled with the bounty of the earth and sea, fiery rubies, cold, twinkling emeralds, and glistening pearls. It was a thing of beauty, but no mere parade weapon to ride beneath the fat belly of a spoiled nawab. The single, heavy, sweeping edge was keen and without blemish, the finest example of Damascene steel they had ever seen.

Even Tishimi, whose swordsmith father had been a master among masters, caught her breath at its gleam.

"I keep it locked away," said Abdul al-Roozbeh. "I know that I will never make another like it."

"How much, master?" Omar breathed, likely more enamored by the gilding than the weapon itself.

"Only the caliph could afford to pay me enough to part with it," said Abdul al-Roozbeh, smiling faintly, and slowly closing the case.

Omar's expression changed as his eyes were denied the weapon's light.

"O grandfather of avarice, why would you craft such a treasure and then miser it away?"

"Don't disrespect the man in his own shop, Omar," Sinbad ordered.

"But why show it to poor sailors like us? Is it not a cruelty?"

"I showed it to Sinbad," said the old master. "Because he is a connoisseur."

Sinbad bowed.

"You do me honor, effendi."

The smith returned the bow and carried his masterwork back behind the beaded curtain.

"Connoisseur," Omar grumbled. "You only got to be so because so many blades have been pointed at you."

Sinbad smiled and turned from the counter, seeing Henri's fingers touching each other, and Ralf's tongue darting slightly across his parted lips. The eyes of his crew followed the old man and his treasure.

They did not see the black clad tough enter at the head of a retinue of ragged looking fighters, the points of naked daggers just visible beyond the cuffs of their sleeves.

Sinbad frowned, threw his red cloak over his shoulders and folded his arms, slipping the throwing dagger from his wide crimson Bhakariot sash as he did so, one hand rising to his ebon face to idly smooth his pointed chin beard and mask the action.

"You are Sinbad El-Ari?" said the leader, with more challenge than civility.

Sinbad nodded as his companions turned and stiffened as one.

"You know I am."

His deep blue eyes, startling in so dark a face, reflected the flash of a half dozen knives as the newcomers pulled back their sleeves with an air of haughty triumph. To Sinbad they had the look and manner of Kohrosan brigands.

"You will come with us," snarled the man in black, brandishing his dagger and gesturing with his free hand for Sinbad to step forward.

"That, effendi," laughed Sinbad, "remains to be seen. Who are you?"

"Who I am is no matter. It is the caliph who has sent me to find you."

"If Haroun al-Rashid sent you," said Omar, "then my father is a monkey."

"Then go back up your tree, chattering, ape!" the man in black hissed. "We are here for Sinbad, not you."

"Now I think you speak the truth," said Sinbad.

"Then you will come?"

"I didn't say that," Sinbad chuckled.

The man in black rushed into the shop with a huff of annoyance, dagger swiping before him in a silver arc. In the next instant Sinbad's knife struck him in the forehead with the force of a javelin and sent him crashing on his back, dead.

"Mind the old man's wares, my friends," Sinbad said, gripping the wood handle of his sword.

"Shop's closed!" Ralf agreed, wild-eyed and grinning. With a roar that had caused blood maddened berserks to turn tail, he plunged headlong into the five Kohrosans, great arms outstretched, heedless of their weapons.

In a tangle of limbs and robes they tumbled out into the thorough-fare, barreling into a pair of palanquin bearers, who dumped their wealthy charge into an outraged butcher's fly-covered stand, spilling a stack of mutton shanks into the street.

There were screams of fear and shrieks of outrage, but all were drowned out by the inquisitive huffing of the trained bear as it caught sight of the piles of meat and began to strain against its leash.

Two of the Kohrosans extricated themselves from beneath Ralf's bulk immediately and jumped to their feet.

Out of the doorway of the shop leapt Sinbad and Omar, their curved sabers in hand, striking almost in unison. Sinbad spun like a black dervish as he came, and the left hand Kohrosan's head went bouncing on the cobbles, while Omar's blade struck low and swept the right hand man from belly to shoulder.

In that time the third Kohorsan had pulled himself free and lunged at Omar's side.

There was a hiss in the air as of a cobra striking, and a trembling arrow shaft pierced the man's forearm. He let out a cry and dropped his dagger. Omar staved in the top of his skull with the pommel of his sword.

Omar looked back and nodded his wordless thanks to Henri, crouched in the shopkeeper's doorway, fitting another arrow into his bow.

Sinbad pulled Ralf up by his fur lined collar. The Kohrosan beneath him had driven his dagger partway into the great youth's side and pulled it free. He was poised to strike again when Sinbad lashed out with his sandaled foot and drove his dagger arm against the stones, feeling the crack but missing the satisfaction of the sound beneath the man's scream.

Omar helped Ralf to his unsteady feet and inspected his bleeding side.

"Arab fools," Ralf muttered, wincing and leaning on the first mate. "Brought dinnerware to a fray."

"And you were nearly the main course, you suckling pig," Omar groaned under the youth's considerable weight.

"Careful," said Sinbad, spying two more men shouldering through the crowd, drawing tulwars as they came.

"Sinbad!" it was Henri, from the doorway.

Sinbad did not hesitate. His mind was as sharp as his blade, honed in years of street fights and actions on lurching decks at sea. He spun, and his steel met steel with a clang. A second pair of swordsmen had moved in behind them. Henri's warning had saved him from a bloodying, but now his sword was locked, and he saw the second man moving in, swinging from the side, a disemboweling cut.

Omar supported the bleeding Ralf. Henri was aiming from the door, but Sinbad himself was blocking his shot.

Sinbad wondered what had become of Tishimi, usually in the thick of a fight like this.

Perhaps he had foolishly overestimated himself and his crew, but not his luck.

As the second swordsman darted in for the killing blow, he was suddenly pulled down screaming by a gigantic furred black form that rose up behind him, taller than even Ralf. It was the bear, broken loose from its master and charging at the aroma of mutton in the street.

The hapless Kohrosan had made the unfortunate mistake of being the only one in the market not to get out of its way.

As the bear stomped across the shrieking swordsman, its great shoulder upset the man Sinbad was contending with. He swiftly slipped the Kohrosan's guard and ran him through to the knuckles.

Omar hollered a curse and leapt away, expecting Ralf, the only one left in the bear's path, to do the same.

But the north man only blinked at the charging bear's approach, balled up his fist, and struck the bear a hammer blow on the top of its snout that sent it crashing to the street as though pole axed. Its head bounced once on the cobbles, then the bear lay still.

Sinbad freed his blade and sidestepped the fallen animal, ready to deal with the last two. He found them lying face down in the street, Tishimi wiping their blood from her single edged sword with one of the pristine white cloths she kept folded in her pockets for that very purpose.

Henri was the first to Sinbad's side.

"Are you alright, capitan? I couldn't shoot for fear of hitting you."

Sinbad clapped a hand on the Frank's shoulder.

"It's alright, Henri. I'm fine."

Ralf smirked at Omar as the first mate picked himself up warily.

"It was just a little bear, Omar."

He held out his hand to the older man.

Omar slapped it away.

Presently the bear's owner rushed up wringing his hands and alternately worrying over the bear's condition and who would pay for the animal were it dead.

Henri stepped to the man, raising his hands and speaking in a placating manner, assuring him his animal was only stunned, and kneeling down beside it to be sure.

"Who are they?" Sinbad wondered aloud as Omar came to his side.

"Not the caliph's men," Omar said. "Kohrosans."

But what were Kohrosans doing in Baghdad, and why had they come looking for Sinbad?

"How are you, Ralf?" Sinbad asked the giant youth.

Ralf shrugged and put a hand to his bleeding side.

"I will mend, Sinbad."

The rich man who had crashed into the butcher's stand was having it out with the vendor. The bear stirred groggily to its unsteady feet as its master fitted its collar about it once more. The usual chaos of the market swiftly returned despite the recent violence, when there came the blast of a horn and the crowd of onlookers parted for a retinue of the royal guard, imposing in their official garb and pikes.

"Sinbad!" called out one of the guards, a one eyed man with a black beard. "I should have known you and your cutthroats would be behind this disturbance."

"Hello, Captain Doud," Sinbad said to the man. "Your men responded pretty quickly for once, though you're still too late to be of any help."

"We were already on our way. To find you."

"What do you want with me?"

"The caliph has summoned you to his august presence."

Sinbad looked at Henri, who had joined him at his side.

Henri raised his eyebrows.

"Truly this time?" he said.

Of the five companions who were ushered by Doud into the court of the illustrious Haroun al-Rashid, Caliph of Baghdad, within the lush Palace of Eternity, only Sinbad, the son of Nubian and Moorish royalty, had ever seen anything approaching its opulence.

Even Tishimi, who had accompanied her father into the castles of daimyo, and once even the shogun, looked on her rich, marble hewn surroundings with awe.

They walked upon Mosul alabaster floors, white as trackless snow, unblemished but for the flicker of the waving torch fires on the tall golden stands.

Splendidly feathered peacocks strutted amid the blue lapis lazuli columns, and straight backed youths bustled back and forth with brimming amphoras and tinkling crystal carafes of cool wine that split the firelight into brilliant prisms. Shapely women, perhaps the models for the lustrous nude shapes adorning the glorious frescos that climbed the ceiling, lounged on plump, ostrich feather cushions in transparent red tunics, their haunting dark eyes lingering appraisingly on Sinbad and his crew. They fluttered bold painted eyelids that caused even the usually unimpressed Ralf to look twice as he passed.

The eyes of Henri Delacrois seemed to appraise every rich furnishing, every golden spangle in the ear of every languorous concubine, and to keep a running tally which spread his admiring grin ever wider until it almost surpassed the points of his mustache.

"One day," he whispered laconically to himself. "One day."

They were led to sit on a series of ebony pillows arranged on a thick, richly woven carpet on the floor, and presently the caliph himself appeared, in the white turban and mournful black robes of the Abbasids since time immemorial. He was strong featured, but there was a trace of fat upon him, like a superb wax carving that had been left sitting in a sunny shop window too long. He was nearly the same age as Sinbad and walked with a gaze more self-assured than outright imperious, but there was a creeping air of haughtiness, impossible for any man to avoid when surrounded for too long by such luxury. Sinbad knew.

Haroun al-Rashid seated himself upon a black divan, and was immediately flanked by two sleek women equal in beauty and form to houri, who fanned him gently with a pair of great purple dyed feathers. He deflected the attentions of a pair of serving boys, and gestured for them to fill the cups of Sinbad and his crew.

Yahya bin Khalid bin Barmak, the sharp nosed Persian vizier, swept into the room in a brightly colored silken robe and took his place before the Caliph on a lower seat. The man was soft faced, with a generous paunch and a curling mustache, too meticulously well tended to impress Sinbad overly. Some said the Barmaks were the real power in Baghdad. Sinbad didn't care to follow the machinations of powerful men too closely, except when it affected his business. But he found he did not like this man.

The caliph waited patiently until each of the visitors had tasted cool, Damascan wine and pomegranate juice, before speaking.

"Welcome, Captain Sinbad El-Ari, and to your wondrous companions."

Each of them nodded their chins in answer, deferring to Sinbad to converse with the royal person.

"This is the second time today we've been summoned to your august presence, lord," Sinbad said.

"Is it?" the caliph said, looking to his vizier querulously.

"Yes, but the first invitation was surely too discourteous to have truly come from you."

"What are you talking about, man?" the caliph frowned.

"Several Kohrosan brigands claiming to have been sent by you accosted us in the marketplace. They claimed you had sent for me."

"Kohrosans. Really?" he said, looking to Doud, who nodded by way of confirmation.

"You see? They are getting bolder, sire," said Yahya.

"Yes yes, Yahya. You were right and I was wrong." The caliph sighed grandly. "Just the other day my son said to me, 'The Persians ruled for a thousand years and did not need us Arabs even for a day. We have been ruling them for one or two centuries and cannot do without them for an hour.'" He chuckled. "Ah, I suppose that's why his mother is Persian. Still. It's a pity. I do love Baghdad."

"Sire?" Sinbad ventured, clearing his throat to bring the monarch's wandering talk back to the business at hand. "Are you planning a trip?"

"A relocation, I'm afraid. To ar-Raqqa."

"Permanently?"

"Yes," groaned the caliph reluctantly. "Yahya and his sons will inherit the Palace of Eternities. I shall expand the royal house at ar-Raqqa. I can keep a better eye on Byzantium and Syria from there. Sinbad, I am beset on every side by intrigues from every corner of the empire. I cannot trust even my own governors. I am spread thin, and have very few friends. There are rumblings of war, spies in my very court. Even my own sons bicker amongst themselves."

He rubbed his eyes tiredly.

"I hope the caliph doesn't think me impertinent," Sinbad spoke. "But what has this to do with me and my crew?"

"Yes of course. Yahya, call for the box."

"Sire," Yahya assented, though with a hint of reluctance. He clapped his hands sharply, and a pair of boys kneeling in the shadows left the room.

"Those assassins you encountered were no doubt hired by one of my enemies. They must have been here in Baghdad waiting about for orders from someone in my court to have tried to intercept you so quickly after I issued the command to Captain Doud here that you should be brought before me."

"And what do you want me for sire?"

"I have been given a plethora of advice on how to prepare for war, Sinbad. I have inventors drawing up plans in the House of Knowledge for all manner of ingenious new devices for killing. I have been advised to step up arms production, to muster slave armies and elephant cavalry and bolster alliances and fortify my cities. Everyone has an opinion on how to prepare for war, but none can tell me to my satisfaction how to prevent war altogether."

The boys returned, bearing a jeweled cask between them, about the size of a cedar stump.

Henri and Omar leaned forward at its appearance, no doubt sharing the thought that if the container were so precious, its contents must be doubly so.

"Ah," said the caliph, as the boys stopped before him and laid the cask at his feet. "But then, while transferring artifacts from the treasury to be shipped to ar-Raqqah, one of my accountants found the answer."

The caliph rose from his divan and the boys retreated.

"Tell me Sinbad, do you know of the sword called the Shamshir-e Zomorrodnegar?"

Sinbad had a vague sense of the name. He was not much of a follower of legends. In his view, a man made his own stories for others to tell.

He looked to his crew, who had only just this morning been arguing like children over the merits of various fairytales and smirked when Omar tapped his lips and stared hard at the caliph, as though he could not contain himself.

"Omar?"

Omar put his forehead once to the carpet before addressing the caliph then said excitedly;

"Pardon this worthless one, but does my lord speak of the Sword of Solomon?"

"Yes," the caliph smiled, pointing at Omar as if he had answered a perplexing riddle to the man's delight. "The Sword of Solomon. It could slay any demon, and it is said that cuts inflicted by the blade cannot be healed, except by a potion made from the brains of a demon called Fuwad-zereh, the general of Malek Khazen, the fairy king of Zahrgiah. Fuwad-zereh was born of a witch, who forged for him a skin of unbreakable steel that turned aside every arrow, and broke every blade, except," and he held up one ringed finger here, "the Shamshir-e Zomorrodnegar."

Sinbad was quiet for a moment afterward. He glanced at his crew. Hen-

"..does my lord speak of the Sword of Solomon?"

ri caught his look and shrugged, perplexed.

"I'm sorry, sire," said Sinbad, clearing his throat "I must ask again. What does this have to do with us?"

"The hero Amir Aslan stole the wondrous sword from Fuwad-zereh and slew both him and his evil mother. But after that, he took the sword with him in a ship and sailed to a faraway island with no name. An enchanted island which no ship could approach. An island of monsters. There he left the sword, and there it is to this day."

He wheeled about, eyes alight, hands grasping at the air in his excitement.

"Can you imagine, Sinbad, what enemy would dare move against me if I possessed such a weapon? A sword which kills with but the slightest cut. It could be a powerful deterrent against my foes."

"Sire, with respect, isn't this….a fairy tale?"

"Hah! I should think the great Sinbad the Sailor should be the last among my servants to dismiss any wonder as pipe smoke or children's fantasies. You, who have in your time tangled with djinn and sorcerers. No matter. I thought it a tale too," said the caliph. "Until my accountants discovered this, hidden behind a wall of my treasury."

He stooped over and plucked off the lid of the cask by its jeweled handle. The two boys rushed in to take the lid from him, but the caliph shooed them away impatiently and deposited the precious lid with a great clang behind him.

Sinbad and the others craned their necks to peer inside as the caliph reached in and with both hands pulled out what looked like an overlarge tarnished metal helmet, horned like the ones Ralf's people wore, with a full, fearsomely carved mask as Sinbad had once seen on a helmet from Tishima's land. The aspect was of a terrible, distorted face, eyeless and snarling through double rows of sharp, copper teeth.

The caliph grinned as he lifted it, then began to strain with the heavy thing and hissed at the boys to come over. They swiftly took the thing from him, each gripping a horn, and he straightened and clapped his hands.

"There, you see?"

"Very impressive workmanship, lord." Sinbad shrugged. "What is it?"

"Why, the head of Fuwad-zereh of course!" the caliph said, exasperated.

"May I?" Sinbad asked, peering at the thing uncertainly.

The caliph gave his assent to approach with a bob of his chin, and Sinbad rose and went to inspect the object closer.

It was no helmet, that was certain. It was quite solid. He took the thing from the two boys, gripping it by the horns, and it was so heavy he hand to bend his knees before setting it with a heavy clang down on the floor. He turned it upside down and peered into the bottom. There was a glistening matter within, similar in consistency to what one might find in the bottom of a severed head, yet darker, more viscous. It was fresh as the day it had been cut.

His stoic face did not betray it, but Sinbad was inwardly astounded. Though he had born witness to many enchantments in his voyages, he had not yet entirely lost his sense of wonder at their infinite variety.

"Well?" the caliph insisted.

"Sire," Sinbad said cautiously. "Are not demons things of fire and air?"

"Ah but Fuwad-zereh was only half a demon! His mother was a witch, remember?"

If this was the head of the demon Fuwad-zereh, then the tale of Amir Aslan was true, and the Sword of Solomon was real.

"You are a believer now, are you not?" the caliph grinned, his eyes hungry.

"I am coming around, sire," Sinbad allowed. "But what about this nameless isle? If you mean me to find it…."

"I would not send you on an endless voyage," the caliph interrupted.

He snapped his fingers at Doud, and the man stepped forward.

"Your sword, Doud."

Sinbad noticed some hesitation in Doud. Then the man relinquished his heavy scimitar to the caliph, who turned, raised it, and brought it down full upon the jeweled cask, making Henri and Omar groan uncontrollably.

As the pretty thing split into two halves, Sinbad saw that the inner lining was a map etched upon a segmented scroll of beaten gold.

Forgetting himself momentarily at the growing prospect of a new adventure, he darted forward and held open the split halves, running his hand lovingly along the finely crafted chart.

"Omar!" he called.

The Sindhi first mate scooted forward on his knees until he was peering over his captain's shoulder.

Sinbad ran a trembling finger along the chart, his sea blue eyes alight, tracing a line from Al-Basra far to the south and east, across the Indian Ocean and through areas fancifully illustrated by coiling sea serpents and fearsome leviathans spouting fire. At the end of the route was a tiny blot of an island, unnamed, but marked with a simply drawn curved sword.

"I do not know these waters," Omar whispered. "No Sindhi does."

"But the route is clear," Sinbad argued.

"To a point, Sinbad," Omar said. "But here," and he pointed to the monster infested area of the map, "there may be nothing but the edge of the world."

Sinbad pursed his lips and slapped his first mate lightly on the ear.

Omar clapped a hand to his offended face, stunned.

"Why did you do that?" he demanded shrilly.

"You'll get worse if ever you spout such nonsense in my presence again."

"I'm sorry, Sinbad," Omar said meekly. They really had sailed together too long for Omar to hold any stock in such superstitions.

"Now, the route is clear, yes?" Sinbad repeated.

"Yes," Omar admitted, still rubbing his ear. "It could be done. But we will need provisions. And we'll be going beyond even the Dibajat. Far south, where none have ever sailed before."

Sinbad grinned, and when he looked up, the caliph was sharing his grin, his eyes hungry. For a moment he thought the monarch was going to ask to come along.

"All the more reason to go," he chuckled, sensing the ripple of anticipatory pleasure echoed in the souls of his friends.

The greatest sea port in the Arab world was Al-Basra, the place where many paths met.

And among the many dhows bobbing in the harbor, the greatest of them all was the Blue Nymph.

She was ostensibly a baghlah, one of the intrepid shallow draft ships whose sharp bows and lateen sails allowed them to outpace the turgid monsoons that plagued the Indian Ocean upon which they plied their prosperous trade. But her type would remain unmatched and unseen in those waters for centuries, for her exact specifications, which some covetous sailors whispered must have been divinely inspired by the Lord of All Waters Himself, were entirely of original design. She had been so heavily modified and refitted under the direction of Sinbad and Omar, that she barely resembled any ship sailing the seas. She was not sewn together with fibers, as was the preferred method among Arabian shipwrights. Her strong Ethiopian teakwood planks were mysteriously joined by twinkling metal fasteners. It was a technique Sinbad and Omar had learned from the Viking shipbuilders, and was practically unknown in this part of the world.

The Blue Nymph's rippling canvas was dyed sky blue, a vanity of Sinbad's, but one which also served to keep all but the most daring of the Bawarij corsairs away as his fierce reputation preceded him. She could, at an order, raise a jib on her bowsprit, or supplement her main from the topmast, and with the blessing of the wind she could attain a speed unmatched.

Her gloriously ornate stern had been carved by a master woodworker and his son for a sultan's ransom. It depicted a beauteous, full bodied, mermaid, smiling impishly, her circling black hair writhing like serpents, as if captured underwater, her scaly tail curling upwards mischievously, as if beckoning her pursuers on. All around her were seven starfish, representing the seven seas her captain had conquered. Her two shining eyes were crystal blue and composed of great globes of inset glass, though some swore they were two great jewels Sinbad had procured in his travels. Whatever their make, they gave the appearance of two mighty nazar charms, twice warding the ship against the evil eye.

To see that flirtatious, mocking smile recede, to hear the crack as the wind caught her lovely blue sails, to see the ocean split before her and to be left bobbing in the white foam of her powerful wake, that was a heartbreak to many a sailor who had never set foot upon her.

But to the twenty five lusty men who sang heartily as they lovingly scrubbed her decks and wove and tarred her rigging beneath the sun, she was the greatest home many of them had ever known. Her captain did not allow just any sea rat to set an unworthy heel upon her decks, and to be a member of that immortal crew was almost to be beloved in the eyes of Allah. No shirkers there, for broad-shouldered Omar would toss a fool overboard by his ear, and to be thrown off the Blue Nymph was a greater curse than to be denied her decks, because who would employ a fool that had attained that august company and been cast out?

No coward either, for all knew that wherever the captain of the Blue Nymph pointed her prow there would be death and danger enough for a fleet of such vessels. But even the most pitiable jellyspine pined for one such voyage with Sinbad the Sailor. All knew men who had returned from his journeys and retired young to lives of luxury, bolstered by unfathomable riches which their generous master always paid out to any who would quit the sea.

But some never quit.

Sinbad and his companions were such. For them, the sea was their greatest love. That boundless blue plain pulled their souls, and would not release them until their bodies gave up the tug of war at the end of their days and the waves rolled over the only graves they would ever know.

There were others too.

Like young curly headed Haroun, a penniless bastard, a son of bastards, with the name of the caliph of Baghdad, who secretly thought himself more fortunate as a member of the Blue Nymph's crew.

The youth sat in a sling dangling over the stern with buckets of paint, touching up the blue and gold gilt work of the Blue Nymph's namesake. He turned and flashed an ecstatic smile at the appearance of Sinbad, striding down the dock like a sable emperor, his blue silken shirt and the embroidered pantaloons tucked into his rich Kurdish boots rippling in the ocean wind, the familiar red cloak billowing out behind him.

Sinbad saw the young sailor at the same time and returned his smile as he reached the foot of the gangplank.

"Ho! Haroun!" he tossed a red apple up to the boy.

Haroun caught it and raised it in thanks.

"How does she look, O Captain?"

Sinbad put his fists on his hips and took in not just the boy's touch up work, but the entirety of his beloved craft. He felt his heart swell within his chest. There was but one thing he loved more than the sea and that was this magnificent craft that carried him across it.

"Beautiful," he answered, and ascended the bouncing gangplank.

Of course Omar was the first man he met upon setting foot on the deck. Sinbad had hardly seen the man since the voyage had been announced. He had taken the caliph's allotment and set about outfitting the Blue Nymph for her voyage, hiring men to replace the ones they'd lost to death and retirement, cramming her stores with rope and blue canvas, water barrels and foodstuffs.

"Sinbad!" he hollered across the naked backs of the bustling hands as he came stomping from starboard to port, fully expecting the lines of hurrying men to get out of his way or be felled by a shivering blow.

"Omar," Sinbad said, knowing well the flustered look on his first mate's face. "What is the matter?"

"Sinbad," Omar said, putting his hands together as if in prayer. "Thou knowest well the delicate balance that must be struck in plotting a voyage of this magnitude, let alone any voyage."

"Of course."

"For every man and," and here he sighed heavily as Tishimi walked by with a coil of rope on her shoulder, "woman aboard there must be made provision. That is why they are called provisions. As worthy a craft as is the

Blue Nymph, sailing is a precise matter. Equal space must be provided for every member of the crew to sleep, to drink, to eat, and defecate…"

"Yes," Sinbad nodded, folding his arms. "I know, Omar. What is your point?"

"Only that should an upset in the balances prevail, we might find ourselves starving or dying of thirst, or without the proper tools to…."

"I know, Omar," Sinbad said again. "Your point, or by the Prophet's beard, I should fetch you a clout!"

"We have a late addition, Sinbad," Omar said, frowning. "An uninvited guest."

"What? A stowaway?"

"Would that it were just a stowaway, Captain. Then I could toss him over the side myself. No, Sinbad. This one bears a signed order from the caliph. He waits for you," and here Omar cleared his throat and looked at his own feet to spare himself the expected wrath, "in your cabin."

"In my cabin?"

Sinbad whirled and without another word marched to the stern. Just as the crew had made way for Omar, though they loved Sinbad more, they did not have to be told to step aside.

Sinbad's cabin on the Blue Nymph was as legendary to seamen as the treasure house of Atlantis. The monstrously large sterncastle was a testament to its opulence, a luxury Omar considered obnoxious, Sinbad thought a well earned amenity, and most captains who wiled their lives away in cramped, leaky quarters sorely envied.

Indeed, Omar jokingly referred to the Blue Nymph's sterncastle as a sternpalace, wherein Sinbad lounged in roomy comfort when not barking orders on deck or steering the ship personally.

Sinbad nearly broke open his own cabin door in his outrage. The captain's quarters were sacrosanct. Even his closest companions didn't enter without knocking, and no man ventured inside unbidden.

He was fully prepared to beat whomever he found behind his cabin door to a paste, but he nearly drew his sword when he saw the rogue testing out his own chair behind his own carved desk, squinting dubiously over his charts.

"Doud!" Sinbad nearly screamed. "Get out of my chair, dog!"

The captain of the caliph's guard actually did rise from the chair in alarm at the unquestionable authority and hint of violence in Sinbad's tone, but he quickly resumed his usual look of superior indifference, angry he had let it slip before the sailor's ire.

"Do not take that tone with me, Sinbad," Doud snarled. "I have the authority of the caliph."

"The only authority on this ship stands before you, Doud," Sinbad snapped, stalking across the room to face him down. "Now get out from behind there. I don't fancy looking across my own desk at any man, least of all you."

Doud huffed, but came around, and Sinbad pulled off his cloak and made a show of dusting his chair before plopping down into it, planting his fists on the arms and throwing a leg brazenly up on the desk.

"What are you doing here, Doud? And when do you leave?"

"I leave when the Shamshir-e Zomorrodnegar is in my possession, and not before," Doud said, fishing a rolled up parchment bearing the caliph's seal. He thrust it at Sinbad.

The sailor glowered and waved him off with his hand.

"Keep your piece of paper," he grumbled. "The caliph might've informed us earlier of his intention to send you along."

"You and your deck apes are being paid quite generously. Besides, do you question the judgment of the caliph?" Doud asked, tucking the scroll away beneath his cloak.

"Does the caliph second guess my trustworthiness?"

"You have a reputation, Sinbad."

"What reputation is that?" Sinbad asked, dropping his foot and leaning forward across his desk. He raised one finger in warning. "Choose your words carefully in my cabin. You have no guards to even your odds, and no man may call me a thief. No matter what certificates he might bear."

Doud sneered, but his jaw muscles worked behind his cheeks.

"My duty is to aid you in procuring the sword, and to insure its return to the caliph," the captain of the guard said evenly, in measured words. "It is known that his majesty's enemies are already keeping a weather eye on you. The caliph wished to send his best man to protect you."

Sinbad leaned back in his chair, smiling wryly.

"Ah? And when will he arrive?"

Doud's fists doubled, but he said nothing.

"Very well. We have no idle hands here, Doud. This is not some rowboat on a pleasure cruise. We sail into unknown waters. Have you any experience around a ship at all?"

"I have my sword," Doud declared, patting the hilt of his heavy scimitar.

"Every man aboard can swing a sword," Sinbad scoffed. "Only sailors walk the decks of the Blue Nymph. The cargo and the kitchen help ride below. Which are you, I wonder?"

Doud stiffened.

"I am no kitchen worker."

Sinbad shrugged.

"Then get below and find a berth and don't let me see you under the sun." He pointed at the fuming soldier. "Most particularly not in my cabin."

Doud gritted his teeth as he turned to leave, and Sinbad put a hand to his face to stifle his own grinning should the man decide to look back.

The cabin door slammed resoundingly and Sinbad allowed himself a chuckle.

Anchored with a landlocked fool he might have to be, but he would be damned if he would let Doud think he was deserving of any special privileges as the caliph's man.

Damn Haroun al-Rashid for his last minute orders. Omar was right. This late in the preparations, it would take some juggling to keep another belly full and watered. Besides that, Sinbad had his doubts about the man's loyalty. He and his men had arrived quiet fortuitously late in the marketplace. Fortuitously, if the idea was to make a show of responsiveness and yet allow enough time for the Kohrosans to fulfill their contracts.

Perhaps the whispers about the Barmaks were true after all, and Doud and the guard really served Yahya the vizier. Perhaps it was the vizier who had ordered him aboard.

Bah, he did so hate palace intrigues. They drove him to intemperance. He reached for a flagon of wine.

There was a knock at his cabin door and it opened, followed soon after by Henri's soft booted step upon the boards.

"What is it, Henri?"

"Sinbad, I couldn't help but hear all that talk about cargo and kitchen help riding below," the Frank grinned. "Surely you don't mean to have me spend the whole voyage down in the hold chopping onions?"

Sinbad flashed a smile. Of all his close companions, Henri Delacrois was the only one with little to no skill as a sailor. Ashore he was a master pathfinder and hunter, but aboard ship he was a tanglefoot and a lubber born. Each of them had taken turns trying to teach him something, anything about sailing, but his was the hand of thumbs laying down catastrophe wherever it fell. Thus he spent every voyage staring out at the waves, whittling, or playing a slim tin flute he kept always about his person.

The newer sailors always began a voyage hating the lazy Christian and ended it praying that Allah forgive him his infidel beliefs and accept him into Paradise when his time came, for his friendship was as true as his aim.

"Did you bring your dice bag?" Sinbad asked, forgetting his annoyance and Doud for the moment.

In answer, the Frank lifted a small green felt bag and shook it, the knucklebone dice clicking about within.

"Come, let me win some of your money, Henri," Sinbad chuckled, clearing aside the stack of charts. "I would rather a slothful Christian with loose purse strings and bad luck than an utterly useless brother of the faith."

The Blue Nymph's azure sails swelled before the wind and the men raised their voices in traditional song as the sleek craft slid from the dock and out into the harbor.

A pair of brown urchins too young yet for the sea raced alongside the ship, dodging roustabouts and cursing fishermen, calling Sinbad's name and waving frantically to catch his attention at the wheel.

Sinbad flashed them a broad white grin and raised his hand to them as they reached the end of the pier shrieking their exuberance and dove into the sea, causing all who saw them to burst into laughter as their heads bobbed up still yelling the legendary captain's name.

The ship sliced into the harbor and Sinbad pointed her south for the open sea, where the clear blue on blue horizon waited.

Omar sidled up alongside Sinbad, frowning as ever, arms folded.

"Listen to them sing," he grumbled. "Are they sailors or a god-cursed bevy of choirboys?"

"They are both," Sinbad laughed grandly.

The loudest of the voices was Ralf's. The Norseman led the chantey in his guttural, halted Arabic, and the sound made Omar frown all the more.

"You are wrong, Sinbad," Omar spat. "They are no choir."

Long after noon a group of islands appeared to the west.

Henri, who by that time had joined Sinbad on the quarterdeck, pointed them out.

"Are those the Maldives?"

"Yes," said Sinbad. "What we call the Dibajat. These are but the northernmost atolls and islands."

"Sails ho!" shouted young Haroun from atop the swaying mast, where he shimmied like a monkey.

Sinbad followed his point and squinted till his eyes watered. The boy had been blessed with an eagle's gaze. A moment later three striped sails appeared, a dhow slipping quickly out from between the turtleback swells of green land.

"Maldivian sailors?" Henri asked.

"No," Sinbad said, wetting his lips.

Omar rushed up the steps.

"Corsairs, Sinbad. Bawarij."

"I thought so," said Sinbad. "But they don't look to be headed our way."

"They would be fools to do so," Omar agreed.

"But what are they doing around the Dibajat?"

"What concern is it of ours?"

Sinbad watched the corsair slink off to the east, bound for Socotra, that haven of pirates, no doubt.

Then Haroun called out at the same time he saw it, "Look there! Smoke!"

Black and inky, rising from the blind spot from which the corsair had emerged.

"Some hapless vessel blown off course, or driven aground by those devils and burned," Omar said.

"Aye," said Sinbad, gesturing for Omar to take the wheel. "Make for it. Henri, with me."

Sinbad and Henri swung down from the quarterdeck and made for the prow of the ship.

"Be at the ready, men," Sinbad urged every sailor he passed.

Tishimi joined them, and Ralf came up behind.

Sinbad informed them of his intent as the horizon spun and the islands loomed before them.

"Pirates," Ralf growled. "I would've liked to have cut a few of them down."

"You may get your chance yet," Tishimi observed.

As the ship neared the islands, they saw a second ship run aground, a small two master.

On the beach there was a group of brightly garbed men in a circle. The black smoke seemed to be rising from their midst, and the wind carried a woman's screams to their ears.

Sinbad drew his sword and swept it once in a circle as a signal to the quarterdeck.

Omar raised his hand in understanding, and the sailors watching tense-

The black smoke seemed to be rising from their midst.

ly in the space between silently moved to their action stations, some of them drawing bright swords or daggers.

Haroun slid down from the mast and ran to fetch his weapons, in a moment returning with white bearded Rafi, the surgeon.

"God give us no need for your talents today, my friend," Sinbad whispered as Omar steered the ship a distance away from the open beach, the scene sliding out of their sight.

Henri strung up his bow and knelt by the bulwarks.

"Only twelve," Henri said.

Tishimi drew her sword and Ralf freed his great rune covered axe.

"Left behind to commandeer their prize," Sinbad said. Sinbad looked back at the crew and quickly pointed to five men. These five grinned savagely and joined them in the fore.

Haroun emerged with his sword. Sinbad turned away to avoid seeing the boy's crestfallen look.

"Your counting is off," Henri said. "It won't be a fair match."

"Not for them," Ralf chuckled. "Stay here if you're afraid, little man."

"You will stay here, Henri," Sinbad said. The Frank opened his mouth to protest, but Sinbad cut him off. "Your bow will better serve us here. While we cross the peninsula, have Omar bring the Nymph around to cover the beach."

"As you say, mon capitan."

Sinbad turned to face the five sailors that had joined them.

"Just a prize crew of Bawarij dogs, O my men. They are nothing to us, but they have captives. We will swim to shore, cross the peninsula through the jungle and take these craven jackals from the land."

The men nodded silently.

Sinbad stripped off his turban, tunic and boots, revealing his dark musculature, as perfectly carved as ornamental teakwood. Ralf followed suit, and though many stole a lingering glance, none raised an undisciplined word as Tishimi shed her voluminous panatloons and crouched in little more than a loincloth and half shirt, the hard muscles beneath her soft pale skin more of a deterrent against lasciviousness than even Sinbad's disapproval.

As the Blue Nymph kissed the shallows, Sinbad gave the signal, and they leapt over the side into the cool water by twos.

They swam like a school of porpoises to the shore and broke at last from the water dripping.

Sinbad looked back once to see the Blue Nymph following his command, then quietly urged his companions into the tangled foliage.

They picked their way carefully but swiftly through strip of jungle, parting fronds and vines before them.

Soon they heard the shrieking of the woman again, heaving out violently in between barely discernible cries and protestations.

Something else reached their senses, a sweet smell of roasting meat.

"I should have eaten breakfast," Ralf muttered.

"What these dogs are serving even a savage like you would not care to taste, my friend," Sinbad said darkly as they came within sight of the beach through the crisscrossing greenery.

The brigands still stood in a semicircle, which was open towards the landward side, affording a full view of their object of attention.

Two figures were staked out in the sand, spread eagled, their fine clothes torn from them and distributed among the Bawarij, heedless as to their purpose. One scruffy pirate wore a spotless silken turban with a glittering opal brooch pin. Another had crammed his fat body into a finely embroidered purple vest until its seams were popping. A third wore ridiculous curled shoes, and a toothless cutthroat chuckled beneath a billowing woman's veil and golden tiara.

Of the two naked figures on the sand, one was an elderly man, and quite dead, his blackened torso being the source of the cooking smell.

A lit brand protruded from his prodigious stomach. Someone had cut him open and thrust it inside. It was a slow, terrible way to die.

Beside him, a fine figured woman much his junior, really a splendid specimen of Persian womanhood, thrashed and wept, tossing her black haired head of springy curls side to side, casting her bleary eyes again and again to the old man, lost in her extreme sorrow. She was completely oblivious to the hungry eyes of the pirates that had turned like bloated mosquitos, their blood lust sated to the point of gorging, from the death they had dealt, and now focused upon her naked form with an altogether different yearning.

They had arrived at the most timely moment for the girl, anyway.

As the first of them prodded her heavy breasts with the toe of his stolen sandal, as the second moved to fall upon her, Sinbad loosed a terrible roar of chivalric outrage from deep in his chest and exploded from the clearing, his lithe dark form crossing the distance in bounds like a charging panther, sword capturing the sun for a brief moment before passing through the stomach of one of the brigands and obscuring the reflection in blood.

Matching his captain's stride came Ralf, bellowing an equally harrowing cry as he plunged into the midst of the surprised Bawarij, hewing down two at a time with his devastating axe.

Tishimi was like a bolt of lightning to the thunder of the Sailor and the Norseman. She dodged nimbly through their midst, sword flashing so quickly on either side of her there was no time for blood to collect on the blade or her person. She emerged at the far end of the group, spun around, and charged over the twitching corpses she had left in her wake to attack the stunned survivors.

The remainder of the sailors attacked without mercy, taking up the cry of Sinbad and Ralf almost in one throat. The pirates that had not dropped dead in the initial onslaught were few, but they reacted quickly, and steel clashed with steel. But the resistance was short lived, and by the time the sailors realized they had triumphed, their captain had thrown a tunic over the Persian woman's shoulders and lifted her in his shining black arms.

He spared them a single approving nod before trudging off toward the grounded ship, his two companions at his side.

Albeit briefly, they had fought beside Sinbad. For the sailors, that was enough.

When Sinbad and the landing party again gained the deck of the Blue Nymph, Doud was waiting for them, looking stern, his arms folded across his barrel chest. Henri and Omar stood on either side of him.

"The sun is yet up, Doud," Sinbad said, setting the silent, shivering woman on the deck and waving Rafi the surgeon over, "why are you on deck?"

"Why have we diverted to these islands, Captain Sinbad?"

Sinbad turned to Rafi and gently pushed the girl to him. She was hesitant to leave his side, but he urged her on.

"Rafi, I do not think she is hurt, but look her over and see. And get her some clothes." To the Persian woman, he said, smiling reassuringly, "Go with the old man, treasure. He may look like an old piece of driftwood, but he studied medicine at the august university. He will tend your cuts and bruises and send you back to me."

She lowered her eyes and shuffled over, letting old Rafi take her by the elbow. She stopped though, and looked back at Sinbad.

"Vanda. My name is Vanda."

Sinbad nodded.

"Vanda then."

She went off with the surgeon, and Sinbad watched her go before returning to Doud.

"Why?" Doud repeated.

"Bawarij pirates. They drove a ship aground, slew the crew. All but an old man and this woman. They tortured the old man to death and were about to set upon her as a pack of dogs before we stopped them."

"You haven't answered my question," Doud said dryly. "Why did we stop here?"

"I have answered your question," Sinbad said. "If you don't understand the answer, that is the fault of your upbringing."

Doud gripped his sword hilt, and stiffened, but Sinbad knew he would do nothing and put his hands on his hips.

"Do not forget your purpose, Captain," Doud said. "You have been paid to reach the nameless isle, not to patrol the sea between. I suppose now you think to return that woman to Basra."

"Don't worry, Doud. We'll be back on course presently. Now get below. The sight of you offends me."

Doud turned in a huff and strode across the deck. No one got out of his way, and he shoved a man aside to reach the ladder to the hold.

"That one," Omar said, watching Doud descend into the hold. "May his manhood wither and drop off."

"You dog, Sinbad," Henri grinned at Omar's side, his eyes not on Doud, but on Vanda as she closed the door of the surgeon's cabin behind her. "I see now why you ordered me to stay aboard. You save the pirate's greatest spoil for yourself."

"She was all that was of worth aboard that ship. Strange that the Bawarij bothered with them."

"The Bawarij would sink the Prophet for the raft he stood upon," Omar spat over the side. "For a woman as fine as that they would do worse."

"You speak truth," Sinbad acknowledged. "But I wonder who her old father was. Or husband, if he was that."

"She hasn't said?" Henri asked.

"She hasn't said anything since we took her from the beach."

"All this talk of women," Ralf groaned, blowing through his lips. "Sinbad, tell them of the slaughter."

"Spawn of savages," Omar said, rolling his eyes. "When I was your age I could talk of nothing but beautiful women."

"When you were my age, old man, all you did was talk," Ralf countered.

"Leave talk of killing for another time," Sinbad said. "Let us return to our purpose and leave that bloody beach behind."

"What of the woman?" Omar asked.

"She goes with us," Sinbad said.

The Blue Nymph sailed on south, leaving the Dibajat to memory. She sailed into the night, across the swelling moonlit waters, with darkness her only companion.

Rafi gave the Persian woman his cabin as sanctuary, and hung his hammock down below with the crew.

In the cabin of Sinbad, the captain feasted and drank with Ralf, Henri, and Tishimi, while Omar walked the dark deck, reading the stars like signposts.

"Why do you drink that bitter tonic from your dainty little cups, Tishimi?" Ralf slurred drunkenly. "You fight like a man. Why don't you drink like one?"

He slammed his wooden tankard on the table for emphasis, sloshing his ale over his forearm.

Tishimi allowed one of her small bowed smiles.

"It seems to me that a warrior's fighting style may be observed in how he partakes of spirits," she said, raising her eyebrows at the dripping mess Ralf had made.

"What the hell does that mean?" Ralf said, blinking.

"She means you fight like you drink, you sloppy barbarian," Henri chuckled.

"Bah! Only a woman would worry about keeping clean while killing," Ralf said, waving his great hand.

He lurched to his feet, overturning his chair.

"I'm going to my hammock."

He stood expectantly for a moment, but expecting what, he couldn't say.

"Good night!" he roared finally. He spared one last look at Tishimi and scoffed. "Bah!"

He went stumbling out onto the deck.

"One day the lad will admit how much he likes you, girl," Henri said to Tishimi when the door slammed shut.

She smiled into her cup as she drained it, then rose and bowed to Sinbad.

"Good night, Tishimi-chan," Sinbad said, as Henri watched her depart.

"And one night perhaps you will tell her the same," Sinbad observed wryly.

"What do you take me for?" Henri said in mock perturbation, raising his cup to his lips. "A blushing boy? I've made my intentions known."

"Have you?" said Sinbad, raising his eyebrows. "And how were they received?"

"That woman prefers the company of her sword to any man," Henri shrugged, downing his wine. "It's too bad really. Those two would probably make the most storied love affair since Tristram and Iseult if either of them could put down their weapons long enough to notice each other."

Sinbad laughed.

"Now what of Doud, Sinbad?" Henri asked.

"What of him?"

"How long will you suffer the one eyed dog's presence? You must know before this voyage is over you will have to kill him."

"You believe he works for the caliph's enemies?"

"You don't? They have tried to kill you once already over this sword business, before you even accepted the job. Do you think they would let the Nymph sail without an assassin on board?"

"Who is 'they' do you think?'"

Henri waved his hand.

"I have no head for Moslem politics. A sultan, a sheik, maybe the vizier himself. What does that matter? We need only concern ourselves with the one who intends to do the deed."

"If it is Doud," Sinbad said, "then he has me fooled. He's a man without guile, I believe."

"Fools are not without guile, they're just bad at it," Henri said. "You think it's one of the crew then?"

"It's hard to believe Omar wouldn't sniff out an assassin. The man is a bloodhound when it comes to picking the rotten apples out of the crew."

Henri yawned and stood, stretching his limbs until they popped.

"Whomever it is, you had better find them before we reach these strange waters."

"Why?"

"I just have a feeling, Sinbad," Henri said ominously as he headed for the door. "A feeling we'll be too busy once we get there to notice a dagger coming from behind."

"Good night, my friend," Sinbad said.

Henri nodded and opened the cabin door.

Vanda was standing there in the moonlight.

Henri smiled back at Sinbad, touched the brim of his cap to the Persian woman, and went outside as she came in.

Sinbad stood and put his hand on the back of his chair.

"I did not think you would be up to dinner, or I should have sent you an invitation." He gestured to Tishimi's place, the neatest at the table. "Please sit."

She stood in the doorway for a moment, then moved around the table and sat down.

He passed her a dish of rice with lentils and goat meat.

"Thank you," she said. "Earlier today, I did not think I would be sitting down to a meal such as this ever again."

Sinbad returned to his seat and sipped his ale quietly, watching her eat. She seemed eager to shovel the food in, but was reserved in his presence. She caught him looking, and dabbed a napkin at her lips self consciously.

"It's alright. We don't stand to ceremony here as you can see," he said, gesturing to the remnants of Ralf's meal and drink spread across his place at the table.

She smirked. It was very nearly a smile.

She was a fetching thing, with a mane of wild black curls she had failed to tame with whatever grooming tools she had improvised in the surgeon's quarters. Rafi had scrounged a plain tunic and white sailor's pants for her. She'd had to wrap a blue sash twice about her waist to keep them up. The roominess could not entirely hide her generous proportions, however.

Vanda. Her very name meant desire.

"If you will permit me to ask," Sinbad began. "How did you fall into such trouble? What were you doing around the Dibajat Isles?"

"My father is….," and she caught herself. Her lips grimaced slightly and she hid her eyes.

He pushed a cup of wine across the table to her.

She took it and drank, set it down when she was again composed.

"My father was a man of science. An apothecary by trade. He hired a ship to the Dibajat to study a certain plant which grew only on the northernmost atoll. He wanted to bring back specimens to test for their pharmaceutical properties."

Sinbad nodded. That explained the lack of cargo aboard the ship. She had not been stocked for a long journey. Sinbad had also found broken jars containing plant matter strewn about one of the cabins. No doubt the pirates had ransacked the old man's belongings and discarded them as valueless.

"Why did your father take you along?"

She stiffened at the question, but then relaxed.

"I was his assistant in all things. He taught me his trade and the sciences."

"That's an uncommon thing for a father to do."

"My father was a very forward thinking man. I can read and do figures. I kept the balance sheets for our shop. Father never had a head for figures."

She had been smiling faintly, and now she looked down into her glass. The smile sank.

"And now he is dead."

"I'm sorry we didn't come across you sooner. We might have saved him. The Bawarij corsairs are animals of the lowest order."

"Yes," she said. "When will we reach Basra?"

Sinbad sat back and narrowed his eyes.

"My lady, we are not going to Basra."

"We aren't?" she asked, with a hint of alarm in her voice. "Where are you taking me?"

"I'm sorry, but we are undertaking an important task, and we don't have the time or stores for a return trip to Basra at this point."

"A trading voyage? Basra is not so far away...."

"It is now," Sinbad said. "And no, this is not a trading voyage. Believe me, if it was within my power to transport you to a safe place I would."

"Then where we're going, isn't safe?"

"I'm afraid not." He held up his hands. "I would not lie to you, who have already suffered so much."

"Where are we going?"

"To an island in the south, to fetch something and return."

"And there is no friendly port between here and there?"

"There is nothing between here and there. Nothing but the sea."

He leaned forward across the table and took her hand in his. It was soft, and quivered at his touch.

"Hear me now. I did not pluck you from those Bawarij dogs to cast you into the maw of death. No harm will come to you on my ship, under my sails. You have the word of Sinbad, lady. You will be with us when we sail into Basra."

She stared at him. Her eyes were quite dark and large. Lovely.

He held her gaze brazenly, and when her hand moved beneath his, he released it and stood.

"Of course my cabin is yours, if you wish to stay," he said, turning his back on her and striding to the curtained corner. He drew his shirt over his head as he went, the bunched muscles in his ebon back and shoulders lean and powerful.

He drew aside the wisp of material to reveal his luxurious canopied bed, inset into a wooden frame in the floor.

He turned to look at her, and cast his shirt on the sea chest at the foot of the bed.

She had been watching his progression the entire time, and now she dipped her head and looked at the table, her cheeks coloring.

"Sir, I...."

There was a rattle as he hooked a hammock to an iron ring in the ceiling near the bed.

He smiled.

"You may sleep in the bed, of course."

"Oh!" she said, blushing again and chuckling nervously into the back of her hand.

He shared her mirth as he climbed into the rocking hammock.

"Relax, treasure. No woman shares Sinbad's bed without her asking."

He yawned and kicked off his Kurdish boots.

"You may leave the dishes for the boy. But please douse the lights before you retire."

He folded his hands behind the base of his head and closed his eyes, leaving her seated at the dinner table, alternately finishing her plate and lingering on his sleeping form.

For weeks the Blue Nymph kept a southerly course. They were well out of pirate waters and far from any shipping lanes. Not a single sail broke the monotonous horizon.

The albatrosses and the gulls dwindled from diving flocks to single wanderers and finally disappeared altogether.

The magnificent ship knew no company but her children and the occasional whale which breached the surface of the rolling waves. The sea was like a blue desert, trackless, endless.

The men amused themselves with games of chance, at the center of which Henri ruled with his green bag of knucklebone dice as a symbol of office.

Tishimi spent her days in the bow, drawing her sword endlessly, and moving dancelike amid scores of invisible enemies, cutting them down in near constant practice.

There was always work to be done, and Omar saw to it that it was done. The man never seemed to rest. He could be found on the deck at all hours of the day and night, throwing a kick into young Haroun's backside or cursing the temperamental wind and weathering spars, torn canvas, and even Allah himself to the dismay of the hands, who clamped their hands over their ears rather than hear such blasphemy. And if they dropped a rope in so doing, woe be it to them. The man heaped ever more heinous blasphemies in their very ears until they returned to their duty.

Young Ralf was the third greatest sailor among them. He had sailed from Novgorod through frozen waters and pulled an oar through icy gales. This southern voyage was very like one of the caliph's boat trips down the Tigris to him, and he often said as much in a loud voice to the annoyance of the Sindhi sailors, who loved the Indian Ocean almost as much as they loved the Blue Nymph. Ralf busied himself about the various tasks of the ship, never tiring.

As for Sinbad, when he was not manning the wheel, for it was one of his greatest joys to do so, he was paying attention to the fair Vanda, walking the deck with her, pointing out the unique aspects of the Nymph and explaining the purpose of various implements on board.

It was quickly established she was Sinbad's woman, almost as quickly established as it was that Tishimi was no man's, and without bloodshed too.

Still, many a hungry eye followed Vanda's walks with Sinbad when the captain had turned his back, and Omar was heard to grumble;

"Women are bad luck at sea."

Though out of Tishimi's hearing.

Sinbad's attention was diverted enough by Vanda that he grew lax in enforcing his law against Doud. The captain of the guard ventured on deck more and more frequently, lurking about, running his fingers idly along the bulwarks and enquiring of Omar again and again about their progress.

"We will get there when we get there," Omar finally said one day. "If the captain of the guard is not entertained, perhaps he would be willing to fill his idle time learning how to be of use on a dhow."

But he was not.

The day came when Omar called upon Sinbad in his quarters, and noticed the hammock that had previously been hung from the ceiling beside his be had been stowed away.

Sinbad sat at his desk frowning over the golden map that had come from the caliph's cask.

"Tomorrow we test the accuracy of this chart, Omar," Sinbad said, tapping his desk with the back of his hand.

"Are you still eager to see the island, Captain?" Omar asked, folding his arms.

Sinbad wrinkled his brow.

"I am more eager to see the chests of gold the caliph has promised us," he said, rubbing his hands together, "but yes, I will be glad to know we haven't sailed down here for nothing."

"The trip has already proved prosperous for you, it seems," Omar said.

"What does that mean?"

Omar shrugged.

"Only that you and your wife shall be able to buy yourselves a fine house to raise children in."

Sinbad stared at Omar and laughed.

"Vanda?"

"You should name at least one of your daughters after the mother," Omar went on. "I usually run out of girls' names anyway. But by the Prophet's blood, don't let the mother find her daughter has been named after another wife."

"It's an honest mistake. Your children can't be easily counted," Sinbad said, rising from the desk. "But I am not you, my friend. Fatherhood, marriage….I do not think these things are for me."

"You can still sail whenever you want," Omar said. "I look forward to the day when one of my boys will be old enough to kick around the deck of the Nymph."

"Nay, my friend," Sinbad said, shaking his head. "Were I to finally take a wife, it would be enough burden to bear without adding children to it."

"Then, my captain, as a father of many daughters, may I ask what your intention with this Persian girl is?"

"Are you her father as well?"

"Thank Allah I am not," Omar said pointedly.

Sinbad paused, then threw up his hands.

"You think I take advantage of her grief? What do you want me to do, old man?"

"Be the captain. Be the Sailor. Tomorrow we weigh anchor at an island of monsters and magic. This is no time to be mooning over some woman.

Sinbad stared at Omar and laughed.

You will be reaching for her instead of your sword, admiring her backside when death comes. For you or for any one of these lustful fools under your command. She is a distraction, and you can't afford them, not when death even now seeks you on this very ship somewhere."

Omar smiled behind his beard then and shrugged.

"Unless you intend to take her as a wife. Then…."

"Then what?"

"I have many wives, Sinbad. And I love them all. I would not lead any woman I loved into hell; not to become caliph myself. If you would give your heart, don't offer it on the end of a blade."

Sinbad stared at Omar and finally nodded.

"I have heard you, old friend."

He took the golden chart from his desk, rolled it up, and slipped it into his tunic.

Sinbad found Vanda standing in the bow, watching Tishimi as she knelt on her woven tatami mat, her sword sheathed at her side, eyes closed; the sea wind rustling the black strands that escaped her bound hair.

Vanda turned as he approached, a full bright smile on her warm face, her own curls whipping about her.

"She doesn't move, Sinbad. Not at all! What manner of woman is she?"

"She's meditating," Sinbad said. "Preparing for tomorrow."

Vanda slid a hand up his hard stomach, but he caught her by the wrist. She frowned.

"Tonight you will go to my cabin and stay there. You will not come out for any reason tomorrow."

"What is the matter?"

"Just get to the cabin," he said coldly, releasing her arm.

She backed away from him, her lovely face nonplussed.

"Have I done something wrong?"

He stepped aside and pointed to the sterncastle.

Her full lips trembling, she raced across the deck.

Sinbad leaned heavily on the mast for a moment, watching the figurehead flying over the unknown waters.

"No, treasure," he whispered. "The offense is mine."

"Omar spoke to you," Tishimi said quietly from the bow.

"Yes. Have you all been disapproving of me?"

"I expected such behavior from the Christian," she answered. Then, before his anger could rise, she said quickly;

"You have done right, Captain. The deck of this ship is no place for a woman."

Sinbad smiled and shook his head.

He spent that night on the quarterdeck, wrapped in his cloak. With his ear to the deck, he imagined he could hear Vanda weeping in his cabin down below.

Dawn rose from the surface of the churning waters like a fiery leviathan bursting forth at the end of days.

It painted over the over the deepest darkness, the total black of the moonless sea, so like the chaotic waters before Creation.

But there was one spot it could not reach, an inky smudge of raining cloud that hovered in the purpling sky and churned the far off waters and cast a great shadow over the sea.

And of course, over the island they sought.

It lay there like a stone in the midst of the waters, dark and defiant, obscured behind a curtain of violent wind and rain. Waiting for Sinbad and his crew.

"Do you see?" Haroun called down from the mast.

"Of course we do!" Omar called back. "Get down from there, climbing bastard of a monkey, before Allah Himself decides to pluck you up and put you in his orchard!"

Sinbad gripped the wheel and stared at the darkness.

"The storm doesn't move, Sinbad," Henri observed. "Does that happen?"

"Nay," Ralf muttered at his side, his lips curling as if he had a bad taste in his mouth. "Magic. Why did it have to be magic?"

"We knew what to expect, prince of animal worshipers," Omar chastised. "If you're afraid, take a barrel and a plank and use your vaunted Viking rowing skill to paddle your way back to Basra."

"One day you will find your tongue laying at your feet, old man," Ralf sighed.

"Tishimi," Henri said. "Your sword is magic. Can't you stand out on the figurehead and cut a hole in that for us to pass through?"

"I can't cut rain and wind, gaijin," she said.

"Take heart, Henri," Sinbad said as they drew so close they could hear the howling, unnatural winds. He patted the wheel of the ship fondly. "We have all the magic we need right here."

And then Vanda was truly forgotten. As was the caliph, and the vizier, and Doud and Solomon's sword and all the petty worries that had gathered during the voyage. Now the infernal wind blew them all away, and the waves that crashed down on the deck, washed them from the captain's mind.

Now it was but Sinbad and the Blue Nymph, commanding a crew against all the fury the tempestuous wall of wind could summon.

No need for a magic sword, the prow of the Blue Nymph pierced the storm like a spear and the deck rocked as if they had run aground against a mountain, flinging the men to the deck. Then the waves rose midway up the mast and crashed down like the thunderous hand of God, raking screaming men from port to starboard and over the bulwarks. The timber groaned and the canvas hung heavy and wet. Then a gust of mystic wind tore the sail to tatters like a flight of arrows.

Sinbad ordered the blue rags slashed down, and the monkey Haroun was the first to leap for the swaying rigging with a hatchet in his teeth. Ralf was right behind, climbing like a bear in steady, measured increments, the spray plastering his long hair to his broad back.

Another torrent of water blasted across the ship, this one taller than the last, sweeping Ralf's legs from under him momentarily and flushing away the man below him.

Haroun straddled a spar and chopped away the sail, and Ralf swung up to the port side and followed suit.

The ship tilted dangerously to port, the spars actually touching the sea, as the heavy sail fell at last and Haroun lost his grip and fell with it.

Ralf's great arm swung out caught the skinny sailor by the seat of his pants.

On the quarterdeck Henri let loose a relieved cheer and looked to Sinbad, grinning, but the captain knew nothing of the drama that had unfolded above his head. His knuckles were pale on the wheel, his teeth bared behind his mustache, powerful shoulders hunched.

"Raise that canvas!" Sinbad bellowed.

With a tremendous swing of his arm, Ralf flung Haroun back to his perch. The two of them caught the hoists and rode them down to the deck, raising the fresh sail with their weight.

The winds battered the Blue Nymph, throwing it back and forth on the waves. Then, as it crested an enormous wave and went sliding down with stomach churning swiftness into what seemed like a bottomless trough, there was a terrible ragged groan from down below. The entire ship shuddered.

They had penetrated into the calm eye of the mystic storm, but in a final act of vehemence, the storm had flung the Blue Nymph against a jagged reef. Sinbad felt his heart sink as the hull somewhere far beneath his feet tore open.

Immediately she began to sink, and the stairway to the hold filled with water.

The crew took to buckets, and Omar led a party of sailors armed with tools diving below deck to patch her as best they could.

Doud emerged spluttering, gripping the mast and heaving sickly onto the deck.

The Blue Nymph limped forward toward the shore of the verdant island, which shone emerald green and snow white sand on the other side. In the center a great mountain rose, the slumbering volcanic progenitor.

The sun shone straight down through a clear hole in the blue sky above. The violent storm that raged all around did so in a perfect funnel of black cloud.

Still the danger was not passed, for stands of great gull-covered rocks littered the harbor, and Sinbad fought the sluggish rudder of the swamped ship to avoid them.

Henri, Ralf and Tishimi came up the quarterdeck steps, their sopping clothes clinging to their shivering bodies.

"From that tempest to this in a span of a few minutes!" Henri exclaimed, shaking himself like a wet dog.

"We are not out of danger yet, Henri," Sinbad said, frowning at the stones.

"We are taking on a great deal of water," Tishimi observed.

"Go and help Omar. He is below trying to mend the breach," Sinbad ordered.

Tishimi nodded and sprinted down to the deck.

Ralf looked after her.

"How many lost in the storm, Ralf?"

"Four," Ralf said quietly.

"Allah receive them," Sinbad said.

"May He not receive us all today," Henri muttered.

Then they saw a strange sight.

Off the port bow, bobbing in the sea was a great white egg, half the size of the Blue Nymph herself.

Sinbad had encountered rocs many times before on previous voyages, and he recognized this huge egg as belonging to one of that ill-tempered species, though it was on the small side. Sinbad craned his neck and peered up at the mountain rising from the center of the island. It was possible the egg could have blown down or been dropped somehow. Maybe it had even been borne through the storm from some other island.

It was entirely covered in a woven net. There were dozens of dark shapes swimming in the water all around it, attempting to tow it.

Vanda, bedraggled and water-soaked, stumbled up the quarterdeck stair and pushing her dripping black hair from her eyes, gasped from the rail.

"Merciful Allah, what are they?"

At first Sinbad thought to order Vanda back down below, but he remembered his cabin was likely a shambles, and with the water rising, she might be safer on deck.

He followed her fearful gaze then, and saw the figures struggling with the netted roc egg turn and regard the sinking ship.

They caught only a glimpse before the creatures, one after another, let out a series of audible hisses that were taken up in the throats of the others. Then they sank as one beneath the waves.

"Perhaps the natives of this island," Sinbad said.

The net released, the egg rolled in the water.

Something scrabbled nimbly on top of it, a naked, hunched figure. One of the inhuman hunters, not content to release its prize so easily. It stood in the sun, its skin a seaweed green in cover, banded with blackish stripes. A long sailfin tail whipped behind it. It took something in hand, a heavy club, and began to pummel the egg, seeking to break it open.

Motivated by some instinct he couldn't quite account for, perhaps his romantic nature sympathizing with the helpless infant, Henri brought up his bow.

His missile flew out over the water and struck the dark green hunter in the base of its spine, sending it tumbling headfirst into the brine.

A great shadow passed over them, dark enough to raise a chill and cover the entire deck. The men screamed and hunkered down uselessly as whatever cast it let out a terrible, hair raising shriek and dove straight down.

They watched in amazement as a huge white eagle, three times the size of the ship, plunged its great yellow, black taloned claws into the water and came up again with the egg in its clutches. The mother roc beat down the air with its massive wings, and the force was strong enough to knock most of the sailors flat on the deck.

The thing rose into the air like an incomprehensible archangel, and Sinbad bristled under its piercing yellow eyes. It circled the ship twice, and even Omar could be heard praying, before it wheeled off toward the mountain, climbing higher and higher until it was out of sight on the far side.

"What a monster!" one of the sailors exclaimed.

"Why did you do that, Henri?" Ralf wondered aloud.

"It was going to kill it!" Vanda exclaimed in Henri's defense.

"It might have saved us the trouble later," Sinbad said. "What did possess you, Henri?"

"I don't know," the archer admitted. "It seemed wrong to let the helpless thing be killed."

"Helpless?" Sinbad chuckled nervously. "Yet a babe and half the size of the ship. Try to make an omelet of that beast and see how helpless it is."

"Well, I do not think it will enamor us to the natives overly," Ralf said.

Doud joined them in the stern, shaking seawater from his dripping hair. "By the Prophet's beard, Sinbad, is this the island?"

"It is," Sinbad said warily, "if the caliph's map is correct."

"Then we must put ashore at once and find the sword."

"Finding that sword will be the easy part," Sinbad said, steering the crawling Nymph past the last of the treacherous stones. "Getting it back to the caliph may prove difficult."

"You sailed us through that tempest alright," Doud said, "will it not be easier to sail out?"

"We may not be able to sail anywhere at all with the state the ship is in," Sinbad said grimly, watching the crew bail water furiously over the side.

Tishimi emerged from the hold, pulling the gasping Omar behind her.

Sinbad whistled for one of the men to take the wheel and dashed down to the deck with Henri, Ralf, and Doud behind.

Omar coughed and rose to his feet as they reached him.

"What news, Omar?" Sinbad asked. "How is she?"

"Her belly has a great rip in it, captain," Omar reported. "I lost two men sealing her. We have taken on a great deal of water. Her bottom is dragging along the reef. We must weigh anchor and effect repairs here, lest the reef rend more holes in her. Allah has made landsmen of us all, curse His ineffable name."

"Don't start that talk," Sinbad chided, "or we may find ourselves truly cursed. We may find timber ashore to refit her. We can build rafts to float them back."

He pointed up toward the fore and ordered the anchor weighed.

As a pair of men leapt to, a sailor leaning curiously over the side hollered in horror.

A pair of webbed, clawed hands, fanning out on the ends of muscled, scaly green arms gripped either side of his face and pulled him overboard.

More such monstrous limbs gripped the bulwark rails.

Sinbad pulled his sword and bellowed;

"Repel boarders!"

Out of the blue sea they came, scaling up the sides of the low riding ship, pulling themselves dripping and hissing to the deck.

They had netted the roc and slipped into the water at the approach of the Blue Nymph, surrounding them beneath the water. Now they had risen to attack.

They were hideous to behold, with long crocodilian faces and golden eyes devoid of humanity and all but primitive reasoning. Their heads, like their tails, were crested with elaborate looking sailfins. Their scaled skin was uniformly green, broken with slashes of black or red or yellow stripes, and pale underbellies. Their hands and feet were webbed and hook clawed.

They bound their thighs and biceps with leather thongs, more to hold weapons in place than adorn. They bore simple wooden crossbows and hide quivers, sharp shell daggers, stone clubs and short spears with strange heads of splayed bone slivers.

As they issued their warlike hisses, they displayed great maws lined with carnivorous teeth.

They fell upon the sailors, almost before the men had a chance to drop their bailing pails and reach for weapons. They flowed onto the deck as the killer waves had.

Beside Sinbad, a Sindhi fell screaming as a short spear flew through the air and stuck in the pit of his throat. The weight of the haft broke off the flayed head, and Sinbad saw that they were the serrated spines plucked from stingray tails.

He leapt over the fallen man, his sword whistling, and struck a charging crocodile man dead with the edge of his blade.

Ralf kicked out with one hide boot and sent an attacking creature flailing back, then brought his massive axe up and down with both hands, cleaving the thing from the top of its skull to the waist. It split apart like some kind of exotic lily before he pulled his weapon free and charged the rail.

Henri leapt backwards onto the quarterdeck stair, and for each step he ascended, an arrow sprang from his bow and sank almost to the feathers in one of the creatures.

Tishimi and Omar stood back to back, turning like dancing partners in perfect unison, hewing down the hissing monsters as they came.

Yet the fight was not entirely theirs. Something like two dozen of the creatures swarmed up the sides of the ship, like frenzied sharks plunging into a cloud of bloody water. The sailors fought bravely, but some had never faced such abominations, and died before they could overcome their terror.

The crocodilians used their tails and wicked weapons to terrible effect, sweeping the legs out from under men and dashing their brains across the deck with their heavy clubs or rending terrible ragged wounds open with their shell daggers.

The deck of the Blue Nymph ran with the blood of men and monsters.

Sinbad spied young Haroun dancing around the mast, parrying the thrusts of a spear wielding creature with a hastily grabbed mop, when a crossbow bolt sprouted from his shoulder and he sank to his knees.

Sinbad plunged through the press, beating aside every weapon that sought his skin, until he reached the mast.

The spear wielder slipped around and straddled the groaning youth, poised to deliver a death blow, but Sinbad struck off its upraised arms and most of its head in one swing and kicked it twitching away.

He spun to look for the crossbowman and spied it taking aim at him in the stern, ducking just as a second bolt stuck in the mast very near his head. He slipped his throwing dagger into his palm with one practiced motion and sent it whirling across the deck, where it struck the crossbow-man in the chest with enough force to send it crashing through the door of his own cabin.

He took a knee and touched Haroun's face. The youth smiled weakly, and then old Rafi was there, his white beard spattered with blood, but not his own.

"I have him, captain!" Rafi said. "Look to the quarterdeck!"

Sinbad did, and saw a trio of crocodilians forcing Henri back to the wheel, behind which Vanda crouched and the sailor he had left behind wrestled with a crocodilian for his club. As he made his way back to the stern, he saw three more creeping over the quarterdeck rail behind Henri and shouted a warning, lost in the din of combat.

Tishimi and Omar heard though, and joined him in hacking their way aft. They sloshed ankle deep in blood and seawater and bobbing corpses, the task of bailing the swamped Blue Nymph having been understandably abandoned.

Ralf was in the midst of a kind of combative ecstasy at the starboard rail, one foot up on the bulwark, swinging wildly with his bloody great axe, knocking the creatures back into the sea and taking off the heads of newcomers that poked up.

Almost singlehandedly he was stemming the tide of boarders on the starboard side.

On the port side, Doud and a few sailors were vigorously forcing the creatures back. Sinbad admitted grudgingly to himself that the one-eyed captain of the guard was now earning his keep in blood.

They reached the stair just as Henri turned in surprise at the attack of three new creatures from behind.

The three that had driven him up the stair swept towards him, but Sinbad gripped the tail of one and pulled him on his belly down the steps, causing his two comrades to stumble and fall back into the waiting blades of Omar and Tishimi.

Henri somersaulted backwards to avoid a crushing blow and rolled halfway down the stair, crashing into Omar.

Sinbad dispatched the one he'd grabbed by the tail and he and Tishimi raced up to the quarterdeck, blades flashing. Sinbad killed his outright. Tishimi's opponent aimed a blow at her and stopped short, hesitating. Tishimi however, did not falter and ran the creature through the belly.

The third ripped open Sinbad's forearm with its dagger, and Sinbad threw a knee into it and drove the pommel of his sword into the back of its head. He sidestepped as it slid limply down the steps.

The sailor he had left at the wheel lay dead where Vanda had knelt, his face crushed and unrecognizable, apparently bitten.

Sinbad heard her muffled scream just as the crocodilian's fanned tail disappeared over the rail. Her cry was cut off by a splash.

He raced to the edge and nearly planted his foot on the rail and leapt overboard, when Tashmi's hand gripped his sash and pulled him back.

"Let me go!" he yelled.

"No, Sinbad!" Tishimi returned, staring into his eyes evenly, as no other woman could. "She is gone!"

Sinbad cast one lingering look down. Nothing broke the surface. He waited as long as he could to prove Tishimi wrong, then turned frowning from the rail. He had promised her she would be safe.

"Look!" Tishimi said.

Tishimi...ran the creature through the belly.

The crocodilians were leaping off the ship, leaving their dead mingled with the crew of the Blue Nymph.

Sinbad felt his heart break at the sight. There were so many.

He touched the wheel of the Nymph. It spun like a child's toy. The rudder chain was broken.

"We must abandon her, Sinbad," Tishimi said.

"They will kill us in the water."

"No, look!" she pointed, and Sinbad saw the rush of wakes as a mob of green fins cut the surface of the water and coursed away from the ship in every direction.

What had caused them to retreat?

Then he saw.

Coming straight at them from the island were two long, high prow canoes, manned with dozens of chanting, naked rowers.

"Now what are these?" Sinbad cursed, leaving the wheel and nimbly sliding down to the main deck.

"Sinbad!" Henri called before he saw his captain.

"I see them, Henri. Who do we have left?"

"The crew is dead to a man," Ralf spat grimly, leaning on his axe. The giant Norseman was drenched in blood. "Only the bonecutter and the scrawny rigging monkey live," he said, gesturing to where Rafi was kneeling beside the delirious Haroun, wrapping his wound in linen. "And him barely."

Sinbad looked to Omar in disbelief.

"All of them?"

"The grim beast speaks true, captain," Omar panted, shaking his head bitterly. "Most gracious Allah has shown them all His much-vaunted mercy today."

"Cease your mocking!" a cut and bloody Doud snarled, coming over. "We will have need of Allah's mercy now, for look."

He pointed his bloodstained sword at the swiftly advancing canoes. Each held a bevy of muscular, fearsome looking tattooed warriors. At least they were men, but what sort?

Sinbad chewed his lip. They were sorely outnumbered now, and not fresh.

"Perhaps not," Tishimi said, descending the stair. "I know these people. Let me talk to them."

Tishimi stood upon the rail and hailed the canoes as they drew alongside, in a language none of them understood, but Sinbad recognized as not her own.

In a few moments, a bullish, muscular warrior whose face was tattooed with dark, circular patterns that rendered his flesh mask-like, gestured for his crew to make room.

In a matter of moments they were loaded into the two canoes, Sinbad with Tishimi, Doud, and Henri, the rest borne in the other.

The canoes pushed off and left the Blue Nymph and her dead behind. Sinbad watched her bobbing sadly as she receded. Her waterline was almost to the bulwarks. She would sink past the quarterdeck in a day or so, a wooden tomb for the brave men that had called him captain. Beyond her, the black wall of the magic storm raged ceaselessly.

Somewhere too, the demon things that had attacked them were likely feasting on Vanda's body.

He thought then for the first time in many days of the Sword of Solomon. No wound inflicted by it could heal, it was said. He swore he would test that power on those beasts as soon as he laid hold of it.

The men he found himself with were strong limbed specimens, naked but for skirts made of tightly rolled flax leaves and jewelry of whalebone and shell. They wore their lustrous black hair long, knotted at the top of their heads, and smeared their tattooed skin with some kind of grease. He noticed too that the swirling body marks were actually stained etchings in the skin, giving their hides both color and texture.

The weapons laid beside the rowers in the carved wood canoe were similar to the crocodilians.' Barb tipped short spears, stone clubs, shell daggers, and wicked looking broadleaf wood clubs, the edges fitted with great white shark teeth.

He leaned forward and spoke in Tishimi's ear.

"How do you know these people?"

"When I left Nippon, I sailed aboard a Korean merchant ship. A few of these people were among the crew. They call themselves Maori. They come from far south of my homeland."

"What are they doing here?"

"They are seafarers, but it is strange to find them so far from their home waters."

"Can they be trusted?"

"As much as any people. They are cannibals, but they only eat their enemies."

From behind him, Henri spoke.

"Let us not make enemies of them, Sinbad."

And from further back, Doud added, "I agree."

Their canoes were swift, and the long rhythmic pulls of the rowers bore them to the snow white shore in almost no time, where a delegation, resplendent in feathered cloaks and headdresses, already waited.

"There will be a welcoming ceremony," Tishimi said. "At some point, a dart or other weapon will be cast down. As our leader, you will pick it up, Sinbad. Do not grasp it by the handle, or it will mean war."

Sinbad nodded, and blessed Allah's mercy for the unlikely providence that had brought Tishimi to him.

As they ground ashore, the burly warrior leapt from the boat and splashed across the surf to the sand. He had a long whalebone staff weapon in his hand, intricately carved, with a feathered, greenstone spearhead on one end and a weighted, bladed knot on the other.

As he reached the front of the small cloaked procession of about ten elders, women, and children, seven more such warriors with similar weapons took their places beside him, turned, and began an amazing performance in unison.

Each warrior took up a hunched, aggressive posture, and began to slap their thighs and strike their breasts, grimacing fiercely. They bugged their eyes and shouted at them in one voice;

"Ka mate, ka mate! ka ora! ka ora!

Ka mate! ka mate! ka ora! ka ora!"

They worked themselves into a posturing frenzy. Sinbad thought the display impressive, and he looked to Henri and Doud as the latter man touched his sword.

Sinbad frowned deeply and hissed at him.

"Do nothing!"

The captain of the guard reluctantly let his hand fall away from his weapon.

As Omar and Rafi brought up Haroun between them, Ralf stared wondrously at the performance.

"It is like the chant of the ulfheonir before battle. What does it mean?"

"They are saying, 'I may live or I may die.'"

Ralf beamed and nodded his approval.

"I like these people."

The three warriors stuck out their tongues in a wild gesture.

"What does that mean?" Ralf exclaimed.

"It means they will eat you, Ralf," Henri mumbled. "Still fond of them?"
"Eat us?" Omar repeated, and had to be shushed.

As the warriors rounded up their chant, the eldest of the men behind them, his face and body crowded with tattooing, drew a feathered dart the size of a man's foot from beneath his cloak and cast it into the sand between Sinbad and his friends and the warriors, who stopped their chanting and stared wild eyed at them, club-staffs poised to strike.

Sinbad stepped forward, never taking his eyes from the largest of the warriors. He crouched, and took up the dart by the middle. Rising again, he tucked it into his sash.

The elder nodded his approval and the three warriors assumed a more relaxed stance and backed away to join the ranks of their people.

A gray headed old blind woman, her eyes like poached eggs, was led forward by a pair of young girls.

She lifted her voice in a haunting song, which twisted and wended through the company.

As she sang, the two small girls left her side and disappeared into the gathering, returning momentarily with a pair of ornate wooden casks which instantly reminded Sinbad of the opulent box that had held the head of the demon Fulad-zereh. He was not surprised when the girls opened the casks and removed a pair of brownish, eyeless heads, richly decorated with facial tattoos like the elder.

Henri started, and Sinbad raised a hand to calm him.

"Peace, Christian. You are not in Paris now."

"Would that we were," Ralf chuckled. "Parisians are most accommodating."

"What deviltry is this?" Henri insisted, ignoring the Norseman's gibe at his native city's constant capitulation to Viking raids.

"Mokomokai," Tishimi whispered. "The heads of respected warriors. Past leaders. The Ta Moko, the facial scars, they attest to the great deeds of their ancestors."

Then, as the old woman's voice began to sink in pitch, Tishimi raised her own voice in song. It was some melody of her homeland, the strange words unlike the Maori woman's, but yet somehow complementary.

Sinbad and Omar exchanged amused looks. They'd had no idea she could sing so. It seemed such a girlish talent for one whom they had seen deal death so unflinchingly.

The duet ended after a bit, and Tishimi bowed her head, as did the old woman, followed by the rest of the Maori.

Sinbad and his companions followed suit.

Then the chief stepped forward and began to speak.

Tishimi gestured for Sinbad to rise.

"What is he saying?" Sinbad whispered.

"He tells the story of his people. They were voyaging when a great storm picked them up and carried them to this stormy sea, into this land of monsters. Theirs was not the first ship to break itself in the magic storm, and the Blue Nymph will not be the last. They are trapped here, and fight an unending war with the....tanihwa."

"That is their name for the creatures we fought?"

Tishimi nodded.

"Since the chief was a boy they have fought the tanihwa. Sometimes the tanihwa were eaten, sometimes the Maori."

"They eat those things?" Omar interjected. "Allah preserve us from the appetites of heathens."

"Sometimes the great white birds came down and carried them all away to the mountain," Tishimi went on. "He says that then, about a year ago, Whiro came to the island and brought the evil knife down from the mountain."

"Evil knife?" Doud repeated, leaning forward eagerly.

"Now," said Tishimi, still translating, "the Maori are dying out. Whiro leads the tanihwa. He kills everyone with the evil knife, which opens wounds that cannot be closed again. He grows stronger. Soon he will break free of the island and destroy the whole world."

The chief finished speaking, and sat down in the sand.

Tishimi touched Sinbad's arm.

"You must speak now. Tell them who you are, and how you came to be here. I will translate."

"I am Sinbad al-Ari," Sinbad said, drawing himself up impressively. "I and my companions have come to take away the evil knife you spoke of. If that means slaying every tanihwa and this Whiro himself, we will do it."

He saw the smiles appear on the fearsome faces, and smiled himself.

"Now you must lay down a gift," Tishimi whispered.

"A gift?"

She nodded.

Sinbad thought for a moment, then reached into his tunic and drew out the ancient golden map drawn in the hand of Amir Aslan. He laid the thing at the chief's feet and rose. He and Omar were blessed with keen navigational senses. Once they had traversed a route, they needed no written record to retrace their voyages.

The chief's eyes widened at the sight of the shining map. He reached down and took it, admiring it, studying it.

Then he jammed it under his arm and moved as if to embrace Sinbad. He clapped his hands on either side of Sinbad's head and drew him close, until their foreheads and their noses touched.

The old chief exhaled into Sinbad's lungs, and Sinbad did the same.

"It is the hongi," Tishimi said at his side. "The sharing of the breath of life. We are welcome now."

"Most excellent," Sinbad said, withdrawing from the chief's greeting. "Now ask him who this Whiro is, and where we may find him."

The chief gestured to the others to come forward. He repeated his hongi greeting with Tishimi as Sinbad waited by impatiently.

The chief said something to her, and she turned.

"First there will be a feast."

Sinbad folded his arms and scowled his disapproval as the chief placidly touched noses with the reluctant Omar, and then each of the companions in turn.

Then the first of the warriors did the same to Sinbad, while the others grinned affably over his shoulder.

Sinbad sighed as the burly warrior blew into his nostrils. They would not find the sword this day anyway.

The Maori feast took place about a mile inward at their village. The banquet was set out by old women upon two of three long tables set in the center of the settlement, before what Sinbad assumed was the chief's house, and Tishimi called the wharenui. It was ornately carved with grimacing squat tiki figures and birds. Only two of the three tables were used. It was true then, that their numbers were dwindling. Only ten old men, women, and children, and seven healthy warriors, including the three that had performed the haka remained.

They ate of the bounty of the sea, fish and seaweed dishes, lentils and lobsters. They were hesitant to try any meat they could not readily identify, remembering Tishimi's statement that the Maori ate the enemy dead, but when she realized their trepidation, she dismissed it.

"They only eat their enemies after a battle, and only the enemies they respect. It is to gain their mana, their spiritual energy."

"Don't earn anyone's respect, comrades," Henri muttered.

"Not that you could, Christian," Omar said between belches.

The old chief was called Waha Akiaki, and of the three warriors that had participated in the haka chant, the largest and strongest was named Hakara, and the other two Eti and Kahakaha. The blind old woman was a kind of spiritual leader, they called Orapa.

Henri paid a great deal of attention to one of the serving girls, a beauteous savage with tattooed lips and big eyes called Akeke. After the second time she filled his cup with the local distilment, he pushed young Haroun further down the bench, despite his wound, and made room for her to sit beside him. She was soon touching his mustache and giggling.

"I noticed the tanihwa use some of the same weapons," Sinbad said to Hakara. He gestured to the carved whalebone staff at his side. "But never those."

Through Tishimi, Hakara answered;

"These are taiaha," he said, picking his own up and touching the carved images of grimacing faces reverently. "Any of us would die before we would see one in the hands of one of those beasts. The spirits of our ancestors live inside these weapons."

"Much like your sword, Tishimi," Sinbad observed.

Tishimi bowed her head. Even after all this time it still pained the woman to think on the fate of her father, and how his last act had imbued his spirit into the blade he had crafted. The blade she now carried.

"Tell us of this Whiro now," Sinbad said, laying aside his plate, "and where we may find him."

"Whiro is a dark god of the underworld. He came from the land of the dead and seeks to escape. To do so, he must kill and devour. With every Maori he consumes he grows stronger. When he is strong enough, he will be able to pass through this ring of storms. Who knows what he will do then. Eat the world maybe. The tanihwa we can fight. With the evil knife, Whiro is unstoppable. He need only cut a man's little finger and they die a slow death."

"For every malady, Allah has appointed a remedy," said Rafi.

"The caliph would not have promised two great treasure chests between you if the sword did not do what he said," said Doud.

"I want to know more about Whiro," Sinbad went on. What does he look like?"

Hakara rose and stood barefoot on the table, pantomiming as he spoke, drawing for them a picture of a giant with a horned head and teeth like the steel of Sinbad's sword.

"Whiro is a monster, four times the size of any man. He has a head of great horns like a bullock, and can kick down a tree. When he comes we flee him as we flee no other. Into the jungle in every direction, to meet again later. If he ever catches us all in one place, he will eat us all. Our weapons cannot break his shiny skin, and he is hot to the touch. He can lay a hand on a bush and cause it burst into blame."

"Shiny skin, shiny teeth," Henri observed, turning his attention from Akeke for a moment.

"Metal? Like the head of the demon in the caliph's storehouse?" Doud wondered.

"Tishimi's sword can cut demons," Ralf offered.

"If he is a demon," Tishimi said.

"Even if he is not, there is some magic at work in him, and cutting sorcerers to pieces is in your line," Sinbad said.

"I will stay close by you, Tishimi," Ralf said, half-joking.

"As if you needed a reason," Omar muttered.

"What?"

Omar only drank from his cup.

"What is our plan then, captain?" Omar asked.

"We seek out this Whiro," Doud answered, misunderstanding. "We take the sword from him by force."

"Wrong captain," Omar said sourly.

"First," said Sinbad, but a tremendous crashing of timber to the east cut off his thought and his words.

Akeke and the other Maori woman began to scream, and the men took up their taiahas and leapt to their feet.

"Whiro comes!" shouted the chief, by way of explanation, as he and his retinue began to rush into the forest in the opposite direction. "He comes! Flee!"

Henri stood, as Akeke tugged at his sleeve for him to follow her.

"Sinbad?" he called.

"Go with them, Henri. Cover their retreat in case the tanihwa are waiting. Rafi and Omar, take Haroun too."

They did as they were told, following the fleeing women and children into the forest, Henri drawing his bow as he went.

Hakara, Eti, and Kahakaha remained behind with the other warriors and Sinbad, Tishimi, Ralf, and Doud.

"Why are they still here, if they can do nothing?" Doud said, drawing his sword.

"It is the duty of the warriors to keep the monster distracted until the people can flee," Tishimi answered, squaring her shoulders and holding her katana out before her.

In the distance, they saw the trees begin to sway, crackle and fall.

"Ready yourselves!" Sinbad said, though he need not tell these to steel themselves, men and a woman of mettle as they were.

The Maori warriors, though they could not understand Sinbad's speech, grimly held their ground, taiahas at the ready.

A huge form came crashing out of the tree line, taking great strides down the center of the little village, battering aside huts that got in its path with the trunk of a tree, smoking in its huge metal fist.

It was indeed a demon. This demon, like Fulad-zereh, was encased in a banded fire red hide of metal, like bright copper and beaten gold. Its curling horns were the color of polished silver, and its tusks and teeth iron grey. The tiny eyes in its monstrous face were polar blue flames. Its frame was muscular in the extreme, rippling arms swinging from thick, sloping shoulders. A glowing red iron collar was clamped around its thick neck, and a broken chain hung down over its broad chest, along with a necklace of human skulls, perhaps a dozen or more, all of them scorched coal black.

It wore nothing but a skirt of glowing red mail. No cloth could touch its searing metal skin, and the metal garment it did wear was superheated, glowing like steel from a forge. Sinbad realized that what he was looking at was a kind of armored suit that allowed the creature of flame within to have a physical form.

And hanging at its side like a dagger was a curved, somewhat plain sword. Yet emblazoned along its length were Hebrew characters, and on the pommel rode a six pointed star.

The Shamshir-e Zomorrodnegar. The Sword of Solomon.

"Do you see?" Doud said, unable to contain himself.

Sinbad hushed him with a gesture.

The lumbering demon came into the plaza before the wharenui and brought its makeshift tree trunk truncheon down on the empty long table, smashing it to splinters.

No one moved, waiting to see what the monstrosity would do next.

"Which of you insects is the sailor, Sinbad?" it boomed in Arabic, in a deep voice that sounded like it came from the depths of a cistern.

Sinbad fought down a shudder at hearing his own name, but stepped forward.

"I am Sinbad al-Ari!" he called up to the giant. "Are you the mighty Whiro?"

"Mighty I am," the beast agreed. "And Whiro is the name these islanders call me by, but it has no power over me."

"And what was the name King Solomon called you?" Sinbad asked slyly. He had dealt with demons in the past, and he knew ways to gain an advantage. The first was learning its true name. "For surely an ifrit who could craft so fine a suit for himself had a hand in the great Temple."

And the second was flattery.

Metal groaned as Whiro shifted and assumed a haughty posture, leaning on his club.

"I was a metalworker in that edifice, and I taught Solomon's smiths and artisans their craft. But you will not learn my name by trickery, sea-rat. Twice before I have gone down that road and never again will I be under the power of any mortal."

"As you say, master of demons," Sinbad said, bowing. "How did you come to be here?"

"Paternal vengeance brought me here, and an unworthy dhow which was smashed to driftwood in the magic storm has kept me. But you have a ship mostly intact. That is why I come to you, Sailor. Your name has reached my ear in times past, and I know that but for Allah in Heaven you are the master of the seven seas. I am no ship builder, no navigator, else I would have built a vessel and sailed from this place long ago. By this time my underlings have towed the wreckage of your ship around to my side of the island, where the water is shallow and the timber more plentiful. You will repair it and I will book passage upon it."

"A business arrangement?" Sinbad said, pretending to think it over, stroking his pointed beard. His heart had leapt at the demon's assertion that the Blue Nymph had been towed into the shallows. He still wasn't sure that even if they could repair it they would be able to penetrate the storm, but at least now there was hope. "What will you pay? I don't take on passengers for free, you know."

"I will give you any earthly riches you desire once we have reached our destination."

Sinbad sucked his teeth and shook his head.

"Pardon, but I would need collateral from one such as you. What about that pretty knife of yours?"

The demon laid a steel hand on the hilt of the blade.

"This you cannot have, for it is to be the instrument of my revenge. It is for seeking this blade that I am even on this accursed rock."

"How is that?" Sinbad asked. "And what is this talk of paternal vengeance? Your father is Allah, and you cannot father children."

"So I thought, until an age ago, when a crafty witch penned me in a fence of surrahs. She ordered me to embrace her, and though it burned her body black and hairless I did. She conceived and bore me a son, part flesh part fire. Fulad-zereh was his name, and a finer son never strode beneath the sun. He was high general to the fairy king, and his mother encased him in a skin of iron and steel much like this one. He was invulnerable to any weapon save one. The one I crafted for Solomon himself to command all djinn, whose steel was forged and tempered in my own burning heart ages ago.

A villainous mortal found it and used it to slay my son and his mother. And I, a formless ifrit, could do nothing but stand by and blaze in hate. But I planned my revenge. I allowed myself to be enslaved by a dabbling sorcerer, an old fool whom I tricked into making this suit for me. Eventually I devoured him, and I hired a ship and made straightaway for this island, where my son's assassin had hidden the murder weapon away like the criminal he was.

Now I have it, and I will return to have my revenge."

"But surely," Sinbad said, rubbing his head, "you must know that the one who wronged you was mortal and is long dead."

"One mortal is as another to one who is eternal. I will smell his foul blood in his descendants, and put them all to the sword." And he patted the weapon hanging from his side. "This sword."

"And then what will you do?"

"Then?"

"Powerful as you are and so armed, it won't take you long to wipe out this man's family line will it? What do you intend to do then?"

"Whatever I please. Perhaps I will make myself caliph," the demon grinned.

"Caliph? That is ambitious."

"I am eternal. My ambitions are equally eternal. But this discussion bores me now. What do you say to my proposal?"

"As I said, I must have some collateral. What else can you offer?"

"What about the Persian woman my underlings took from your ship this morning?"

Sinbad's façade of playfulness dropped instantly.

"What do you mean? She lives?"

"For now. My warriors never kill women outright, though they often die in the end. They use them to propagate their corrupt line, for there are only males among them. A peculiarity of their race. She has a generous body. She is prized. Coveted."

"Have they....?"

"Not yet. I have confined her within my own chambers, where they dare not enter. But by dawn their lust will overtake their fear of me. I can give them one of these islander girls if we come to an arrangement before then. If not...."

The demon let his sentence trail off meaningfully, and grinned a hideous grin.

"What say you now, Sinbad al-Ari?"

"I say," he said, slipping his throwing dagger into his hand, "that our negotiations are over. And that Tishimi had better be ready."

"What?" Whiro said in real confusion.

Then the dagger was whipping up at his eye. He batted it aside easily. It clanged off the back of his hand and went off into the jungle harmlessly.

But he did not notice Tishimi put one foot on the table and spring into the air, her father's katana sweeping out before her as she sailed towards the demon's chest.

Whiro pivoted at the last possible moment, and the sword pierced his armor at the shoulder.

Instead of a spray of blood, a gust of blue flame burst from the wound, blowing Tishimi back.

She fell in a heap on the ground. Her sword was still in Whiro's shoulder, blue fire seeping like blood from around the blade.

Whiro howled his outrage and raised his foot to squash Tishimi like an insect.

Ralf, Hakara, and Eti charged the upraised foot and grasping the bottom, upset the demon's balance and sent him crashing onto his back.

The three of them leapt back grimacing and shaking their shoulders and arms. Wherever they had touched Whiro, their skin glowed an angry, bubbling red.

Sinbad and Doud raced forward with the remaining warriors and swarmed over Whiro.

He was impossibly hot to the touch. Sinbad could even feel the heat through his sandals, and the Maori were barefoot. They shrieked and leapt off almost as soon as they'd clambered on.

"Doud, the sword!" Sinbad yelled, gesturing at the glittering weapon hanging from the demon's belt.

The captain of the guard lunged for it, but the demon rolled, first trap-

...the sword pierced his armor at the shoulder.

ping his arm, then bringing his tremendous weight fully to bear. Doud screamed as the crushing, burning giant came down on him. Then his voice was lost in the snapping of his own bones.

Sinbad tried to hold on to something, but could not command his fist to close on the blazing hot surface. He was thrown, but landed on his feet and beat back the demon's groping fingers with his sword.

The warrior Kahakaha was not so lucky. Whiro's hand enclosed him and lifted him. Kahakaha screamed the entire time, his bare skin sizzling in the hot metal grip. Then with a sickening crunch, Whiro clenched his fist and cast the broken body away.

He stumbled to his feet and retreated into the jungle, snarling, his heavy footsteps shaking their bones, leaving deep smoking imprints wherever he stepped.

"After him!" Sinbad shouted.

The order was not required. Tishimi picked up the dead warrior's taiaha and she, Hakara, and Eti ran after Whiro with the other warriors in tow and Ralf bringing up the rear.

Sinbad glanced once over his shoulder, wondering how Henri, Haroun, Rafi and Omar were faring. But he couldn't wait, and plunged into the jungle to follow the smoldering wake of the demon.

The sun slipped behind the lone mountain and the sky darkened. Their pursuit was dogged. The Maori were admirably tireless. They leapt over fallen logs, scrambled up woody hills and down moss strewn valleys, splashing through trickling creeks without slowing, though their physiques shined with sweat.

Whiro had likely not been wounded or felt pain in many a century, and thus he had panicked at his first reminder. Though his immense height had put him far ahead, the signs he left behind were ones of desperation. He made no bones about smashing through trees rather than dodging around. Perhaps he thought that if they had wounded him with one enchanted weapon, they might perhaps have another.

His carelessness had unwittingly paved their way. They had no need to pick through dense brush. The demon had ploughed it all down and left it smoldering in his wake. It was as if they chased a streaking meteorite.

At last they came to the edge of the jungle and spied a vast calm lagoon reflecting the moon on its surface. In the center of the lagoon was a tall hut of stone which glowed from within like a hearth, and on the far side, the sad looking Blue Nymph sat low in the water, attended by a great convocation of wrecked ships hailing from various lands, most of them not more than a few broken masts protruding from the water.

Many visitors had apparently come to the island over the years. By the looks of it, none had left or even remained except the Maori. There were odds and ends taken from the ships strewn all about the lagoon, half submerged. Bits of furniture. A ships' wheel. A rusty, barnacle encrusted anchor and chain.

As they paused for breath in the shadows, Sinbad heard an all-too familiar scream. Whiro came striding out of the hut soon after, eyes and the wound in his shoulder blazing blue. Tishimi's sword was in one fist, Vanda dangling by the ankle from his other, shrieking as her leg sizzled in the demon's grip. Her wrists were bound with clinking chains, her dress torn to mere shreds. Whiro dumped her unceremoniously on the shore of the small island and raised Tishimi's sword and plunged it down. The blade sank nearly to the hilt through the hole in one of the links, pinning her to the ground, where she lay whimpering, clutching her burned ankle.

"Now, Sinbad!" the demon roared out into the night, drawing the Sword of Solomon. "We will discuss new terms!"

Sinbad started to break cover, but Tishimi grabbed his elbow and pointed.

The surface of the lagoon began to ripple and break, maybe a hundred stones rising from the depths. No, not stones, the long, finned heads of the taniwha, their yellow eyes shining like fireflies.

This was their home.

"Sinbad will advance alone and weaponless. His companions will return to the village. Else I will bite off this woman's head."

"Sinbad?" Vanda called out desperately into the dark, and Sinbad ached to hear her call his name.

He looked at Tishimi and Ralf, and began to unstrap his scimitar.

"What are you doing?" Ralf hissed.

"What I must," Sinbad said bitterly.

"What's your plan?" Tishimi asked.

Sinbad shook his head.

"No plan. Return to the village. Save yourselves."

"We'll wait," Ralf insisted. "We'll find a way."

Sinbad handed his sword to Tishimi, nodded to Haraka and Eti, and stepped out of the brush to the shore of the lagoon.

"Here I am, demon!" Sinbad called, holding out his arms and turning to show he was unarmed.

"Make a path!" Whiro roared.

Obediently, several dozen of the silent taniwha swam to the center of the lagoon and lined up, floating to the surface so that they made a living bridge from the shore directly to the island in the middle of the lagoon.

"Step lively, sailor," Whiro ordered. "There is work to be done."

Sinbad hesitated at the shore, then placed one foot on the head of the nearest creature. It was like walking on a floating plank dock. Precarious, but firm.

He made his way slowly along the creature's leathery back and moved on to the next, like a boy traversing a creek by way of stones.

The walk along the bobbing creatures was nerve wracking, for on either side of the makeshift path the other creatures waited, sometimes yawning their great maws like waiting crocodiles.

The demon loomed on the far island, the whimpering Vanda at his feet. She sat up at the sight of him, and seemed to gain strength, rising up on her hands like a seated cat.

Then Sinbad caught a hint of motion from a quarter he had not expected. Out among the ships' graveyard where the Blue Nymph lay, a pair of low shapes moved noiselessly through the water among the broken hulks.

Sinbad slowed his procession, making a show of regaining his balance, putting his arms out and swaying.

"Be careful, sailor," Whiro chuckled deeply. "It would not be wise to fall in the water among them. The splashing agitates them. And they are hungry."

Sinbad crouched and stared ahead, panting as if from fear.

The low shapes moved to the beach on the far end of the lagoon. Several shadowy figures clambered out and pulled it over the sandbar, slipping it into the lagoon water.

Maori canoes. He recognized the silhouettes. But the warriors were with them.

He made another show of nearly falling, splashing the water with his foot to keep the taniwhas' attention.

"Where are your vaunted sea legs, Sinbad?" Whiro taunted.

"Sinbad, be careful!" Vanda pleaded.

Sinbad wondered if Tishimi and Ralf or Haraka or the other Maori had spied the newcomers.

He was very near the island now, but he went slow to give his would be rescuers time.

Whiro loomed on the shore, tall and gleaming in the dark, the blue fire from his eyes and open wound casting Vanda and the island in a cold, mystic light. The neverending storm could be heard pounding in the far distance. Tishimi's sword caught the blue glow, the wavy pattern on the blade made Sinbad think of the open ocean beyond the storm ring.

"No more dawdling, Sinbad," Whiro snarled, putting the swept point of the sword near Vanda's throat.

She gasped.

He wet his feet in the lagoon and walked the rest of the way up onto the island.

"Good," said the demon, slipping the sword back into the braided loop that suspended it from his belt.

He reached down and pulled Tishimi's sword from the sand, and flung it out into the dark where it splashed somewhere in the lagoon.

"Now you may take your woman inside. Tomorrow you will begin work."

Sinbad went and crouched by Vanda, helping her to stand.

He glanced over and saw a burly shape emerge quietly from the water and creep low behind the hut, taking a sword from between his teeth. It was Omar, stripped to a breechclout, the best swimmer among them all.

Sinbad pressed Vanda's cheek to his chest to keep her from giving Omar away with her eyes.

"Sinbad...I thought I would never see you again," she sobbed.

"There now, Treasure," Sinbad cooed, picking her up off her wounded foot and carrying her toward the stone hut. "We're together now, aren't we?"

He reached the threshold with her when he heard the telltale hiss of an arrow.

It was an impossible shot, made in the dark, only the low blue glow of the demon within the steel body to see by, and taken from a bobbing canoe, but Henri Delacrois was no ordinary marksman.

The arrow hissed and parted the simple cord from which the Sword of Solomon hung at Whiro's side.

The shining sword slipped from off the metal giant's belt, but before it struck the sand, Omar was running, spry and fleet for his age and girth. He dove and caught the sword, rolling away from the surprised demon and flinging the magic weapon to Sinbad as he did so.

Sinbad swung Vanda's legs down, and pivoted. He reached out and snatched the surprisingly light and well balanced blade out of the air.

He held the blade before him and glared at Whiro.

"New terms again, demon," Sinbad smirked.

"Kill him!" Whiro bellowed in outrage, backing into the surf.

Instantly the taniwha swarmed the little island. Three died with arrows in them before they had risen entirely from the water. The canoe with Henri in the bow shot across the lagoon, women and children at the oars.

The taniwha that had formed the living path began to turn and rise out of the water, but from the far shore, Ralf bellowed;

"SINBAD! SINBAD!"

The giant Norseman surged from his cover and ran right out across the backs of the bewildered creatures, followed closely by Hakara. They actually managed to get halfway across the lagoon before Sinbad saw the two of them falter and plunge into the water, rolling and hacking at the clawing, snapping taniwha as they fell.

On the far shore, Tishimi, Eti, and the rest of the Maori plunged into the surf and engaged the closest of the crocodilian creatures, Tishimi with Sinbad's sword and the Maori with their taiaha and shark tooth clubs, the latter roaring lustily to match the taniwha's inhuman hisses.

Omar fell back to the stone hut, slashing at the onrushing creatures.

When he reached the doorway and stood shoulder to shoulder with Sinbad, the two formed an impenetrable wall of steel, cutting down the amphibious creatures by the score as they poured so thick onto the little island as to blot out the sand with their blood and carcasses.

The Sword of Solomon was unlike any blade Sinbad had ever wielded, better balanced even than Tishimi's master katana. It took almost no effort at all to heft and swing, and every cut was deadly, passing through the bodies of the creatures entirely, separating them into halves, quarters, breaking through bone as easy as a hatchet through kindling.

Sinbad saw Whiro wading into the lagoon, turning away, glancing in confusion over his shoulder. He quickly advanced over the ground made uneven by mutilated corpses, carving through hordes of the thrashing, hissing monsters until his own limbs were dripping with their blood and he had hacked a clear path through to the steel giant.

"Whiro!" Sinbad called.

Whiro only roared in answer. He stooped in the water and came up with the broken, seaweed covered figurehead of a ship that had long ago broken itself against the magic isle and been borne into the lagoon. He heaved it with one arm at Sinbad.

Sinbad dodged aside and it crashed into the water behind him.

Three of the taniwha tried to surprise him, springing out of the water, seeking to drag him down. He took off all three of their heads with one great sweep, and kept coming.

The water around Whiro's knees boiled and hissed angrily, causing steam to rise all around him like fog.

The demon freed the rusty anchor and chain Sinbad had spied earlier from the mud and began to twirl it over its head, letting out the slack, making a deadly whirling circle around himself that several of the unwitting taniwha fell prey to, the iron anchor smashing in their heads or crushing their bones if they wandered too close.

A few times the demon reached out, testing Sinbad's guard. The anchor should have snapped a regular sword in half, or sent Sinbad flying into the water sideways, but every time it connected, a great blue flash of sparks rose up from the blade. Once an arm of the anchor snapped off entirely.

Sinbad grinned and came closer, keeping his guard up, smacking the demon's strikes away as if they came from a child.

Still, the demon kept backing into the deeper part of the lagoon. Soon Sinbad would be swimming.

Then the monster would have him as a disadvantage.

All around, the battle raged in the frothing water. Maori warriors surfaced screaming as the teeth of their savage enemies worked in their flesh. Others clambered aboard the canoes and dealt death with their taiahas on the creature that tried to pursue. Sinbad glimpsed Ralf holding open one of the taniwha's toothed jaws, pulling it wide, seeking to tear the beast's jaw free. Both factions shrank from the circle of whirling iron in which the two champions faced each other.

Whiro leered and moved into waist high water.

Sinbad stopped, feeling the edge of the downward slope with his toes. Now the demon could strike, but Sinbad could go no further.

Sinbad raised the Sword of Solomon with both hands over his head in a high guard.

"Now our negotiations are at an end, little sea rat!" Whiro said.

He lashed out with the anchor chain, the huge rusty iron weight coming straight at him.

Sinbad spun and cut downward as the anchor sailed past. The enchanted blade parted the chain.

Then he raised the sword again, only higher, the back of the blade nearly touching the small of his back, and lunged forward, releasing.

The Sword of Solomon whipped forward like a spinning wheel of steel. When it stopped, only the Star of David pommel protruded from Whiro's chest.

The demon stumbled backwards. Its blue eyes flashed bright enough to illuminate the whole lagoon, causing all the dark, struggling shapes to blink in confusion and look back. Everyone saw the steel giant give a shudder. Then the light in the demon's eyes winked out and he fell to pieces, clattering apart like a poorly stacked pile of pots and pans.

Whiro had met his end, but the battle had not, and Sinbad found himself in the water with no weapon.

Then one of the sleek Maori canoes came towards him, and there was Henri, crouched in the bow, his arm extended.

Sinbad leapt clear of the water and Henri swung him up into the canoe dripping.

Henri's tattooed beauty Akeke was rowing just behind them. She flashed Sinbad a smile as he picked himself up.

"That was a mighty throw, Sinbad," Henri remarked, picking up his bow.

"And a good shot from you, my friend."

Henri grinned roguishly and nocked an arrow.

"Keep close. You'll see a few more before this night's over."

In the morning the lagoon was choked with floating carcasses, mostly taniwha.

The Maori dead were carried out, as was the Sword of Solomon and Tishimi's katana.

The flies descended upon the rest.

When they had returned to the village, Henri explained that he, Omar, Rafi, and Haroun had accompanied the women into the jungle and double backed to the shore, piling into the canoes to affect the rescue they knew Sinbad would surely need.

The old blind woman, Orapa, had taken the younger children and headed for the mountain.

Haraka set out to find them and returned with the children, but the old woman was not to be found. One of the young girls claimed the great white bird had taken her in the night.

The Maori mourned their dead and the loss of their spiritual leader, when Rafi came up to Sinbad with a frown on his face and took him aside.

"Captain, I have....ill news. It's Omar."

Sinbad found Omar sitting at one of the feast tables, staring at the grimacing carvings on the wharenui.

He had a bandage on his left hand. It was soaked with blood.

"How is it with you, old man?" Sinbad asked quietly, sitting down beside his old friend.

"These tiki things mock me. They are ugly. It is fitting that Allah decree they be the last sight I see. He was ever vindictive to me, though I have fathered many new worshipers for him."

Sinbad looked down at the blood soaked bandage.

"How did it happen?"

"When I threw you that God-cursed sword. I cut the edge of my hand, just there. A tiny little cut. I thought nothing of it. But look. This is the second bandage Rafi has swaddled about it. It slows, but it will not stop I suppose."

Sinbad looked at Rafi.

The surgeon shook his head.

Omar caught sight of the exchange and rolled his eyes.

"This one and his 'Prophet Medicine.' A fine thing an education is. Just a lot of mummery."

"How long?"

"At the rate he is bleeding, tomorrow morning," Rafi said.

"They could have taught you bedside manner."

"Would you rather I lied to you?"

"I would rather you didn't speak to me at all!" Omar snapped. Then he turned back to the Maori carvings and lowered his head. "I am sorry, Rafi."

At that unheard of show of remorse on the part of the grizzled first mate, Rafi's lips trembled and he turned and stalked away.

There was a commotion from the side of the village, but one of mirth, not sadness.

The old woman, Orapa, had stepped out of the jungle unharmed.

The children swarmed around her, laughing and jumping.

She herself beamed and spoke animatedly, gesturing up towards the mountain.

Tishimi came over, excited.

"Sinbad!"

"What is it?" Sinbad asked miserably.

"Orapa says she was spared on the mountain by the roc-mother. She says it was the kindness of the newcomers that spared her. The great roc told her that in gratitude for saving her egg, she will take us all off the island when the sun sets."

Sinbad looked around at the Maori. Unquestioning of the old woman's story, they were already bustling about, apparently gathering their belongings while Haraka and the men went to outfit the long canoes for a sea voyage.

He had personally never known a roc to show any kind of intelligence, and attributed this to wishful thinking on the old woman's part.

"Even if it were true," Sinbad said, "we couldn't make the voyage. There is not enough time to repair the ship."

Tishimi bowed.

"As you say. Haraka and the other warriors say they will tow the Blue Nymph away from the other wrecks anyway, and return it to the bay."

Sinbad shrugged.

Waha Akiaki parted from his hurrying people and came before Sinbad, bearing the golden map that had led them to the accursed island. He extended it to Sinbad, and spoke for some time.

"He asks to return this to you, out of thanks for delivering them from the island. He says that when the great bird drops them on the other side of the storm, they will return to their ancestral islands in the east. He regrets that they are pressed for time, or he should bestow Ta Moko upon us all personally, to commemorate our great deeds and to make us all more attractive."

Sinbad forced a smile and accepted the gift.

The chief grasped his head, touching foreheads and noses and exchanging breath, then turned and went off to help in the organizing effort.

Sinbad stared down at the thing, at the reflection of his dark face in the gold.

He handed it to Tishimi and went off to be alone.

Vanda found him. They enjoyed each other's companionship, but did not speak until much later, in the haze of the afternoon, as they lay staring up through the fronds, the sun making the canopy leaves glow like emeralds.

"You are far away," Vanda remarked, stroking his broad dark chest. "Have you returned to Basra already?"

"My friend is dying. Many times I have led them into danger, into death. But I have always led them out again. Too many have died for this cursed sword. How many more will die?"

"All who sail with you must anticipate life or death, Sinbad. For most, it is why they sail with you. Life is best lived in the midst of death. If they did not know this, if you did not, you would not be Sinbad."

"He is a father. Many times over."

"His share of the caliph's reward is enough to feed and clothe fifty children for life. His widows will want for nothing."

Sinbad sat up and rubbed his head.

"Of course, you are right, my treasure."

He rose and dressed.

"Let us go make ready for this bird."

"You believe the old woman?"

"I disbelieve nothing until it fails to come to pass."

The Maori raised a cheer when Sinbad reappeared and joined in the work of patching and baling the Blue Nymph. Their canoes were outfitted with bundles of food and fresh water, enough for a long journey east. Their work finished, they had turned to the Blue Nymph without question or command, allowing Tishimi to direct their efforts. Though they knew not the workings of the strange vessel, they responded quickly to instruction, and adapted well.

When Sinbad set foot on deck again, she was washed clean of blood and bodies, and the water in her hold was receding.

He went to inspect the hole and came face to face with Omar, who looked pale and hollow eyed, but smiled thinly.

"You should rest in my cabin, old man."

"Not until you've changed the sheets," he quipped. His words were bold, but the voice was tired.

"I'm serious," said Sinbad, gripping the man's upper arm. It was cool to the touch.

"I would see her sail again, Sinbad. Just once more."

Sinbad nodded and let him go.

"Out of the way, Ralf, you great infant!" he snarled, and the Norseman stepped aside to allow him to pass.

When he turned to Sinbad, the giant's eyes were red.

"It's true then?"

"Yes," said Sinbad quietly.

"He called me by name," Ralf said, by way of explanation.

At the approach of nightfall she was not ready to storm the seas, but she rode higher in the surf, and she stared defiantly at the wall of tempest that had wounded her. The Blue Nymph was ready to face her again.

But perhaps the confrontation would not come, for at nightfall, with the Maori gathered on the sand, the enormous white roc came spiraling slowly down from the top of the mountain.

As the huge shadow passed over them all, Sinbad and his companions touched their weapons, but the Maori stood unafraid, even the little children.

"Can it really be?" Henri whispered.

"If so, we have you to thank," said Sinbad.

The huge beast landed on the sand, folding its massive wings, and cocked its great wild head expectantly, shrieking once.

The Maori took this as a signal and piled into their canoes. Akeke embraced Henri before she joined her people.

The happy children waved to what remained of the Blue Nymph's crew, and the warriors raised their taiahas in salute, then stowed them and took up the oars and a chant.

Orapa recited a wailing blessing, or else a farewell serenade, they didn't know which, and as the two canoes left the shore, the huge white bird beat its wings, kicking up a cyclone of white sand and took to the air.

It swooped down then and took up the canoes, one in each massive claw, and climbed ever higher.

They heard the diminishing cheers of the people. Then the bird and its burden could be pinched between two fingers. It sailed over the lip of the magic storm and was gone.

"A miracle," Omar scoffed. "Now at last, I see a miracle."

They took a raft out to the Blue Nymph and climbed aboard, still a bit dubious that the roc would return.

But it did return.

Henri laughed and shouted as it appeared high in the air. It folded its wings and dove straight at the ocean, piercing the surface of the water with a colossal splash.

They looked at each other in confusion, and then the Blue Nymph gave a violent lurch.

"Grab onto something!" Sinbad yelled.

And then the Nymph was flying.

Port and starboard they could see the magnificent white wings of the creature beneath them beating the air. The deck slanted sharply, and the air grew cool as they soared over the island.

Sinbad could see the many wrecked ships near Whiro's lagoon down below. Then he could see the rim of the storm funnel, and then they were over, and the wide blue sea was all around.

The roc dove down and he thought the Nymph would be dropped into

"I would see her sail….once more."

the waters. Down below he saw the two Maori canoes shooting east, and fancied he could see the people waving, tiny as they were.

But the roc did not deposit them. It flew out across the ocean, headed north.

"Lower the sail!" Sinbad ordered, and Ralf took out his axe and cut it down.

The great bird's speed increased noticeably, the wind roaring in all their ears.

"Where is it taking us?" Vanda shrieked above the wind.

Sinbad looked to his compass, checked the heading, and laughed, in spite of everything.

"To Basra, my treasure! With all speed!"

The others laughed too. Even Omar.

Sometime after midnight, in Rafi's quarters, Omar fell asleep and would not wake.

"Will he awaken?" Ralf asked.

Rafi shrugged.

"Who can say? The wound will not close. His body cannot replenish the blood fast enough."

"Then his only hope is that we can reach Baghdad," Henri said. "The brains of Fuwad-zereh."

"This beast will likely drop us in Basra if anywhere," Ralf said. "If only we could speak to it, as old Opara could. Sinbad, what can we do?"

"Pray," Sinbad said, after a bit. "To whatever god will whisper in the ears of a roc, if there be any."

He turned and left them all at Omar's bedside.

He walked the empty deck silently, the roaring wind causing his pantaloons to flap against his legs. He gripped a rope in the prow and leaned out to watch the rushing ocean beneath the ship, the moon overhead. How long and how far would this thing carry them? Perhaps it would tire and set them down far south of Basra yet.

He fancied they were near. He had spent most of the night as the others had, keeping vigil over Omar, and had no real notion of where they were, though he thought he had seen the Dibajat pass by earlier.

That made him think of Vanda sleeping in the stern cabin, and the words Omar had had with him concerning her.

Omar. How many voyages had they sailed together? Sinbad was god-father to every one of his numerous children, and Omar himself was the second father of this very ship. Now he lay dying upon her.

Sinbad folded his hands together and touched them to his forehead.

"By all the wonders I have seen, and by Allah who in His wisdom made them. O great mother of rocs, deposit us not in Basra but in Baghdad, at the palace."

He had no idea that at that same moment a similar silent prayer passed through the minds of Haroun and Rafi, or that Henri had taken a knee at Omar's bedside and invoked his Jesus, or that Tishimi had touched the sword of her father and asked him the same. Even the great Ralf had gripped his axe and spoken the names of Tyr and Odin, though not being one for prayer, he had asked only that the old man not suffer the humilia-tion of the straw death, so that they might see each other again some day in the halls of Valhalla.

Then Sinbad retired to his cabin.

The Sword of Solomon lay upon his desk, carefully wrapped and bound in reeds.

Vanda was sitting there looking at the handle with the six pointed star on the pommel. It was relatively unadorned for an enchanted blade, but its craftsmanship was undeniable.

"It's such a beautiful thing," she said, as Sinbad came to stand over her, "to cause such pain, so much death."

"Yes. I was thinking the same thing," he said stroking her hair.

She guessed his intention.

Her hand came out from under the table, the dagger flashing, seeking his throat. But her wrist met his hard hand, and he balled his fist in the tangle of her hair and drove her head quickly into the desk.

She moaned, the dagger slipping to the floor of the cabin.

Doud, Allah accept him, had never been the assassin. He was too much a fool to be anything other than what he was.

When she had suggested earlier that day that Omar's share of the re-ward would be more than enough compensation for his family, everything had coalesced in Sinbad's brain.

In all their time together, he had never discussed the caliph or the re-ward with her.

When she awoke, she was bound to the raft they had used to reach the Nymph from the shore of the island, and he had her balanced on the bulwark.

She shrieked.

"You cannot do this!"

"Can't I?" Sinbad retorted. "You murderous hussy. Did you hire those Bawarij we encountered at the Dibajat? Who was the old man they burned alive to lure us in?"

"No! He was not my father, but he was the closest to a father I have ever had. He raised me from an orphan, taught me my trade."

"The trade of a hired killer? A seductress?"

"We had planned to fake the sinking of our ship so you would rescue us. The Bawarij surprised us. You did save my life."

"And was it your gratitude that spared me this long?"

"I would only have taken the sword. I had already decided not to kill you."

"What would your masters have said to that?"

"Please. Sinbad. I will tell you who hired me…."

He let go.

She wailed as the raft slipped over the edge of the rail and plummeted down towards the speeding ocean.

There was no splash. He had tied the raft to the anchor.

He leaned over the edge.

She was still strapped to the raft, which now dangled just over the water, far down below.

He took out his knife.

She shouted something up at him. It could have been an entreaty. It was likely a curse.

"Farewell, Treasure!" he called, and parted the line.

The raft splashed into the water, submerged, and surfaced again, bobbing. She quickly disappeared, a small pale form in the dark water behind them.

He had left her dagger on her hip, along with a clay jug of water.

He could see the lights of Basra only a mile or so to the north. If the tide carried her there, so be it. If not…..

So be it.

He went back into his cabin and picked up the sword.

Such a perfectly made weapon. Yet not so impressive a thing to look at as the jeweled sword they had seen in Abdul al-Roozbeh's shop. He ran his fingers over the Hebrew characters on the guard and the six pointed star on the pommel. Yet this weapon was a hundred times more deadly and thus a hundred times more precious. The caliph had promised them enough riches to buy a fleet of ships like the Blue Nymph.

He returned to the deck. His first thought was to throw it overboard. No man should have such power over life. Certainly not Haroun al-Rashid, who though he was not a bad caliph, was not entirely a good man either. Better than his vizier, to be sure, but could a weapon like this once in among the avaricious backstabbers of the court remain long with one owner? The caliph swore he intended to use it to prevent war, but eventually it would fall to someone with lesser intentions. One of his bickering sons perhaps.

Sinbad walked to the rail and thought hard, when he noticed that the waves below were no longer shimmering, no longer rolling.

They were not waves at all, but dunes!

And the city of Basra was falling quickly behind them.

They were sailing over the open desert. Still headed north.

He gave out an excited cry.

Rafi's cabin opened and Ralf, Henri and Tishimi came out onto the deck.

They saw what Sinbad saw, and each gave thanks to their own gods, not guessing they were one and the same.

The great white roc raised the alarm of all Baghdad as it settled at the gates to the city, but among the soldiers, many recognized the Blue Nymph as it slid from the monster's back, and held their weapons until it gave a great ear splitting shriek and took flight once more, leaving blowing dust and a legacy of legends in its wake before it momentarily blotted out the moon and then disappeared somewhere between the early morning stars.

Four figures rushed down the gangplank with a fifth carried between them, and the guards escorted them to the palace at a run, unaware of the nature of the urgency, but bowing to it unquestioned.

No one noticed a sixth man who slipped over the side of the wondrous ship and made his way down the dark avenues.

In the Palace of Eternity, Henri Delacrois balled his fists as the caliph's guards crossed their pikes before the cask containing the head of Fuwadzereh.

"What do you mean you do not have the sword?" the caliph demanded.

"Sire, Captain Sinbad even now brings it to the palace," Henri explained.

"Why did he not come along with you?"

"There was an assassin on board," Henri said, sparing the flustered vizier an appraising glance before he continued. "She sought to take the sword before we reached Baghdad. Sinbad thought it prudent to deliver it by another route, one that did not attract so much attention, in case the villainous cowards decided to make a last ditch attempt."

He directed the last at the vizier himself, with secret delight.

"Well, then we shall just have to wait until he arrives."

"Your highness!" Tishimi pleaded, touching her head to the floor. "Our companion has been gravely injured by the sword. We must prepare the cure, or he will die."

"Really?" the caliph said, leaning forward on his divan. "How fascinating. May I inspect the wound?"

Ralf jumped to his feet, kicking aside the ridiculous cushions and pointing angrily at Omar, who lay on a bier behind them, chest slowly rising and falling.

"Damn it all! He is dying! Give us that demon's brains or...."

The guards stepped forward menacingly.

Rafi covered his head with his hands. He was no fighter.

"Stop!"

The voice came from the hall, and all turned to see Sinbad striding in with an oblong bundle.

He went directly before the caliph and laid the bundle at his feet, unfurling it dramatically.

The caliph's eyes widened, as did the eyes of all the companions, though for entirely different reasons.

The caliph came off the divan and picked up the sword, admiring its sweep and opulence, its jewels and pearls and golden accents.

"Ah! Here is a worthy weapon! Do you see?" he exclaimed, waving it at the vizier, who retreated noticeably. "Just let us see what those jackals do, once word of this reaches their long cur ears. Eh, Yahya?"

Sinbad did not pause, but slapped aside the still crossed pikes of the guards and reached in and took the metal head of the son of Whiro.

He overturned it and carried it to Omar's side.

Henri and Rafi moved to assist him Rafi cutting away the bandages on Omar's hand.

"What of Captain Doud? Is he not among you?"

"He was killed," Tishimi answered.

"Ah?" the caliph said, still admiring the blade. "Well, he was a fine soldier. A fine, fine soldier."

Sinbad rose and stood before the caliph again.

"What of our reward, sire?"

The caliph glanced at him.

"I thought we would have a celebratory banquet. The girls would dance. You would regale us with the tale of your adventure."

"I regret I have not the time, great one. I have pressing matters. My ship lies out on the sand and I must hire laborers to get her into the Tigris before vandals strip her. There are also repairs I must affect lest she sink to the bottom."

"Very well, Sinbad," the caliph said, obviously disappointed.

The caliph clapped his hands, and four slaves entered bearing two huge treasure boxes on long poles between them.

"But you shall owe me the tale."

Sinbad directed the slaves to follow him with a wave of his hand.

He bowed once to the caliph. He glared at the vizier. He paused to look over Omar, Rafi and Henri.

Rafi looked up.

They had rubbed a gray-blue salve into the wound.

"The wound has closed," Rafi said, amazed.

Sinbad nodded.

"Bring him to the river if he lives," said Sinbad, and strode out of the court with the slaves and the reward tromping behind.

Ralf, Tishimi, and Haroun stood, bewildered.

"Sinbad?" Ralf called.

"Stay here, Ralf," Sinbad called over his shoulder.

Then he was gone.

In the morning, they found him by the river, shipwrights and carpenters swarming over the Blue Nymph.

Omar was still on the bier, but he sat up when he saw his captain.

"Could you not even remain at my side, O pernicious father of trickery?

You are like the disciples who slept in the garden while the carpenter to whom the child of infidels bends his knee waited to die."

"You don't look to be dying," Sinbad remarked. "And I haven't slept." To Ralf and Henri, who were bearing Omar between them he said, "Get this noisy cargo aboard. We sail downriver for Basra and then the sea."

"You gave the old swordmaker's masterwork to the caliph," Henri said.

Sinbad nodded.

"And our reward went to paying old Abdul al-Roozbeh."

Tishimi smiled.

"He would accept only a caliph's ransom, he said."

"He and his children need never work again," Sinbad agreed.

"But....I saw two treasure boxes," Omar said. "Or was I dreaming?"

"What remained will go to the widows and orphans this bitter adventure has made. And the golden map paid for our repairs....after I scratched the island from it."

"So we are right where we started," Henri chuckled.

"We are," Sinbad said, ascending the gangplank, "unless the caliph decides to test his prize. Then our names will be worth less than they are now in Baghdad."

"But Sinbad....," Ralf ventured. "What did you do with the real sword?"

Sinbad smiled. He had sealed it in a false plank in one of the new bulkheads below deck. It would remain in the belly of the Blue Nymph until they were far out as sea, then, one night he would go below and cast it over the side.

But no man, not even the true hearted Norseman, need know that.

"It is where no ruler or warlord or demon will find it, Ralf. A weapon like that, perhaps even the wisdom of Solomon failed in its crafting. Now let's be off. I've a first mate and one sailor on the mend and just the four of us to handle the Nymph till we can hire on a new crew in Basra."

"Three, accounting for that layabout Christian," Omar muttered from the bier as they carried him up the gangplank.

Henri's end dipped a bit, nearly spilling the first mate into the river.

Omar gripped the sides and laid a curse upon the Frank and all his descendants.

THE END

THE MOST REMARKABLE EXTRA-ORDINARY FELLOW: HOW I SET SAIL WITH SINBAD

When Ron Fortier put out the call for Sinbad stories, I had a full plate of work on the table.

But I still felt compelled to respond with a tentative 'lemme take a look at the series bible (that's the pre-established document that the publisher keeps which prospective writers refer to for things like character traits, relationships, descriptions, etc.).'

Ron sent it to me, and reading through it, things started to click in my mind. His concept for Sinbad was not to ground the characters entirely in the Arabian Nights mold, but to sort of toss in all these disparate voyagers from different cultures and make them into Sinbad's core crew. There was Ralf the Viking, Tishima from a samurai family, Omar the Sindhi, and Henri the French archer. It was sort of like a 9th century Star Trek bridge crew in its diversity, and that's really what got me to put a hold on other projects and say 'yes I'd like to take a crack at this.'

The way humanity encounters and responds to each other in terms of culture is something I like to visit in my writing. I'm fascinated by the interplay of cultures completely alien to each other (and my own), and I'm delighted when they find a commonality in which to work together.

For Sinbad and his crew, the commonality is adventure and riches, as it should be in any classic adventure worth the read. Sure each character has their own personal motivations and quests, but as a crew, they're after that horizon and the gold that burns there.

The other draw to writing a Sinbad story was Sinbad himself. The name just evokes silken fantasy and curved swords, veiled women and minarets.

The first time I heard the name Sinbad The Sailor was likely the Max Fleischer Popeye cartoon where Bluto played the titular role. In that short, Sinbad was a bit of a jerk. But I remember thinking how cool his island hideout was. He had all these wild animals and monsters kowtowing to him, including a giant buzzard that Popeye of course turns into a huge turkey dinner replete with cutlet frills and platter.

Later I saw the Harryhausen movies, because after I saw Clash Of The Titans and Jason And The Argonauts, I pretty much hunted up anything with that man's name on it. But even then I was in it for the monsters (I once met Ray Harryhausen after a screening of Clash at the 1929 movie-house I worked at in college, and got to see the miniatures for Medusa, one of the Argonauts skeletons and the Cyclops from 7th Voyage up close). Sinbad sort of took a backseat in those pictures, as did all the human actors in a Harryhausen movie (with the possible exception of Burgess Meredith). He wasn't even always played by the same guy!

So I found I didn't know a lot about Sinbad. I had read the first volume of Arabian Nights, but the character doesn't appear there.

In the series bible though, Ron mentioned he envisioned Sinbad as being of partly Nubian descent. I had recently read Changa's Safari, the Conan-esque adventures of a band of roving adventurers related winningly by Milton Davis' pen. In my mind, I conceived of this Sinbad as perhaps an ancestor or distant relation of Davis' intrepid 15th century warrior prince, Changa.

Add to that the fact that I'd been wanting to try my hand at old school pulp sword and sorcery adventure since I first picked up a copy of Hour Of The Dragon, and that I have a deep, abiding love for Thief of Bagdad with Sabu, and I couldn't not try my hand at a Sinbad story.

What sprang from this was magic swords and steel suited demons, crocodile men and Maori (because shark tooth clubs and taiahas are awe-some), and in what I hope was my most Harryhausen-esque creation, a gigantic white roc with a sailing ship on its back.

I love learning as I write. I didn't know Sinbad or the court of Haroun Al-Rashid going in, but the setting had always intrigued me, and I think I came to know them pretty well.

And like any man who looks with longing across the waves, I'm proud to have sailed with Sinbad for the time I did.

EDWARD M. ERDELAC is the author of the acclaimed Judeocentric/ Lovecraftian weird western series MERKABAH RIDER (TALES OF A HIGH PLANES DRIFTER, THE MENSCH WITH NO NAME, HAVE GLYPHS WILL TRAVEL, and ONCE UPON A TIME IN THE WEIRD WEST) and DUBAKU from Damnation Books, as well as BUFF TEA from Texas Review Press , COYOTE'S TRAIL from Comet Press, and TERO-VOLAS from JournalStone. His fiction has appeared in several anthologies and magazines, and he wrote the definitive story about boxing in a galaxy far far away for Lucasfilm's STAR WARS franchise. In 2009 he wrote, directed, and produced and independent film, MEANER THAN HELL.

A Hoosier born, he was educated in Chicago and now lives in the Los Angeles area with his wife and a bona fide slew of kids and cats.

More info can be found on Facebook or at http://emerdelac.wordpress. com.

A Detour for Sinbad

by Erwin K. Roberts

Ralf Gunarson woke to the heavy rumbling of his stomach. He had no idea he would fight for his life before he could eat. Now fully awake Ralf rose and headed aft just in time to see Sinbad el Ari, his captain, sit up in his hammock strung along the Blue Nymph's railing. His left foot checked the deck for moisture, as there had been fog during the night. Assured of firm footing Sinbad now fairly sprang to his feet. Although he had a spacious bed in his aft cabin, the captain often enjoyed spending the night on the deck of his beloved ship.

Ralf headed aft on the other side of the mast, for his captain preferred to compose himself before dealing with the list of things needing attention on just about any day at sea. Sinbad stretched and bent. Even in the half dawn light the muscles on his chest and arms could be seen standing out from the deep, almost chestnut, color of his skin.

Without looking Ralf could picture what came next. Sinbad would open the protective case clamped to the mast to look into the polished bronze signal mirror. He would not like what he saw. His turban needed re-wrapping, badly. But worse, his neatly trimmed chin hair pointed almost directly at the port side horizon.

The captain would head down to his cabin to put things right. Ralf half smiled to himself. Captain Sinbad's wish to greet each new day well groomed, if possible, told nothing about the man himself. Sinbad was strong. Not as strong as Ralf, but he moved much faster then the Norseman. He could use almost any weapon well and was smarter than any man aboard; also a born leader thrown into the bargain.

As Sinbad lifted the hatch to go below, Henri Delacrois, whose homeland the Blue Nymph had departed only the day before, shouted from the bow, "Spar or mast! Floating in the water five points to starboard. About two cable lengths away. Not just bare wood, Captain. Might be worth a look."

A bit of an ironic smile flashed across the captain's face. He turned to the three men helping the cook get the fire started. "Men, dip the starboard side of the sail. Then haul me aloft."

With that Sinbad stepped to the mast. On the aft side he put his bare foot into a spliced loop at the end of a rope that ran to the top of the mast. The rope then returned to the deck to pass through a pulley. A knot kept the resting coil of rope from pulling through. The crewmen finished hauling the top starboard corner of the square sail's yard down as far possible. Now they hurried to the coil of rope. Soon the loop of rope carried Sinbad briskly up the mast.

His eyes rose above the now triangular sail. He caught a glimpse of Tishimi Osara sitting cross-legged in her usual space by the prow. Then he looked outward.

Omar, Sinbad's second in command, stuck his head through the hatch to the deck just as the captain's voice thundered, "There's a man clinging to the far side. Tiller, turn to starboard!"

Before his feet touched the deck again Sinbad began giving orders. The hands rushed to release four of the great oars. Three times the height of a tall man; these would be reversed and used to prevent damage to the ship by the debris. Tishimi helped with the sail handling, he noted. She more than pulled her weight. And the men respected that, though some still maintained having a woman in the crew begged for trouble.

Now the bow of the Blue Nymph eased up to the floating mast. Having checked the ship and crew for readiness Omar, the master Sindhi mariner, moved to the side of his captain. As he scratched his gray beard his eyes darted everywhere.

"Even after the taverns of Gaul the crew has embraced being at sea again without trouble, my friend," observed Sinbad.

"Thus far," came the reply. "This man's own gods must have forsaken him. Decent weather has been ours for a fortnight, yet his ship has broken up. I see signs that some of the heavy ropes snapped."

"I saw that, as well, Omar. Now, who gets to take a bath? You, or me?"

Omar growled. Any of the crew within hearing turned to muffle their laughter. For the First Mate swan like a fish, but only if necessary. He out swam Sinbad just as the captain out swam everybody else.

Sinbad's fingers brushed his disheveled chin. He nodded to himself. "Stay dry, old friend."

With that Sinbad stripped to his clout. This revealed the small dagger strapped to his calf. He headed forward. As he approached the railing Tishimi Osara fell in beside him. In her strangely accented Arabic she said, "There is magic hereabouts, Captain." Her right hand pointed the hilt of the long sword she called a katana.

The gesture was an invitation seldom given. He touched the hilt very lightly with two fingers. He felt vibrations, just barely.

"Thank you, Tishimi. Could he be carrying charms or potions?"

"I do not know, Captain. But I doubt he is in any condition to use such."

"On that we agree. If I had not seen him change his grip on a rope while aloft, I'd have thought him dead."

Now Omar called out the string of orders that lowered and furled the bright indigo sail. Velocity came off the Blue Nymph. She glided to a virtual stop just within safe distance of the debris.

With that Sinbad took a spliced loop from a crewman holding the long coil of rope. He vaulted the railing to splash feet first into the salt water.

The water closed over Sinbad's head. He forced his eyes open. But there was not yet light to see possible snags around the floating debris. So the Captain swam wide to approach the castaway from behind, not across the mast.

"Ho there," called Sinbad in the language of the Franks. The man's body tensed up a bit, but he did not answer. Perhaps he was a Moor, so he added, in Arabic, "Greetings, oh waterlogged one."

With that he pulled himself up to the mast. This was not likely a Moor, thought Sinbad. His skin had been light, before the sun turned it a deep red. Sinbad could see that he wore some sort of cloak with a hood. But under the cloak? A humpback? Sinbad had met a few, but never with a deformity that followed the full length of a man's spine. Something must be under there.

"Can you speak?" he said in Arabic while pointing to his mouth.

Words worked their way around a swollen tongue. Sinbad shook his head. The man tried again. The same words, but clearer this time. The language of Rome!

Though he was not fond of that form of speech Sinbad learned it because so many spoke it.

"Ave, friend. I am Captain of yonder ship. I'm sure you will like our accommodations better than your present ones. We will make better time if you let me tie that thing on your back to my rope."

"That is not possible, Captain. Please let me explain..."

※ ※ ※

From the rail of the Blue Nymph Omar muttered under his breath, "What in the name of a djinni are they doing? Telling jokes?" Then he noticed the exotic looking Tishimi Osara standing next to him. He tried not to jump, for the young woman moved like a shadow.

"As I told the Captain," she almost whispered, "there is magic present."

For all she didn't belong on the ship, Omar knew she rarely opened her mouth without something important to say. And most of the crew stood by the rail watching the Captain. He called out four names.

"You four stand by to raise the sail. The rest of you spread out on watch. We will not get caught with turbans over our eyes!"

"So you see, Captain, I failed in my duty to protect what is now strapped to me. But I recovered it. On the way home a storm came out of nowhere. The ship broke up in a moment. Had a rope connected to the mast not tangled around my arm I would be at the bottom of the ocean. And I will gladly go there before I lose touch with my burden.

"There is magic, yes. It is a conduit only a chosen may use. If anyone else, even I, attempt to use it, death, and much worse follows. I must return my burden before the summer solstice, or innocents may pay the price. Can you help me, Captain Sinbad?"

"Solstice is but a few days hence. But we are in no great hurry. Our only cargo is some hardwoods. Perhaps we can help you. Now, slip onto this loop of rope and I'll guide you."

Omar sighed with relief as Sinbad towed the castaway around the end of the mast. The spliced loop of rope went around the man's body. And each arm wrapped itself around the loop to prevent him from slipping through. Sinbad aimed his strokes just aft of the curve of the bow.

Then came Ralf's strident shout, "Omar! Straight beyond the the debris. A wake! I can't see what's making it. Headed right for us. And fast, too."

Omar's head jerked up. Then he saw it too. His mind flashed back to his childhood. Some friendly enemies tried to sneak up on his skiff breathing through thin reeds. He did not see their bodies under the water, for they used the sunlight and shadows to hide themselves. He could not make out the reeds, either. But they left a mark in the water like the letter the Greeks called Lambda.

Back in the present Omar knew something he could not see, something very big approached. And at the speed of a sprinter going all out.

"Raise sail!" he bellowed. "Three men, pull in the line. Carefully, so he doesn't slide out. Ralf, retrieve the Captain. An oar, rope, however you can. Henri! Get weapons passed out. Tiller! Soon as we clear that mast, hard to port! Move you sons of camels!" To those unfamiliar with the operation of a sailing ship chaos reigned on the deck of the Blue Nymph. Omar continued to shout oaths and encouragement, but he knew his crew. Order would quickly emerge from the chaos, if only there was enough time.

Sinbad saw the sail begin to rise. An instant later he felt the first tug on the rope. He let go assuring the castaway he would soon be on deck. Then he struck for the side of the ship. As he reached it a rope ladder splashed down. One of the sailors swarmed down to help the other man.

"Captain, reach up" cried a voice from above him.

Sinbad looked up into the close face of another of the crew with his arms outstretched almost to the lapping water. Sinbad raised his arms. He shook off what water he could, then grabbed the crewman almost at the elbows. The other's hands locked around his arms in roughly the same places. Then both men rose, as if by magic. A moment later Ralf Gunarson lowered the two men to the deck. Sinbad got his bearings just in time to help get the castaway over the rail.

"Hard to port... Now!" thundered Omar. "Aeieih! Allah does not like us, today. It's turning into us."

Sinbad sprang to Omar's side. "What's turning?"

"Hades and Pluto if I know, Sinbad. See that wake?"

"Indeed! But what..."

"Nothing good, I'll wager. Here, take your sword and dagger... Wait! The head of the wake has disappeared."

"Might be diving. Could come under us."

"Grab hold all!" cried Omar. "We may get rammed!"

A split second later the ugliest thing ever seen by the crew of the Blue Nymph rose up from the water just forward of the mast. And kept rising. Big around as an African water buffalo, it's gleaming scales made a rasping sound as they scraped the ship's side and the railing. The creature rose ever higher.

From where he lay on the deck the castaway screamed one word, "Stoorworm!"

The creature's dragon-like head looked down on the scrambling humans. Then the thing recognized the castaway. The sinuous neck bent almost double as the snouted head seemed to dive for the deck and the exhausted man. The creature's mouth began opening. A forked tongue darted out.

A goose fletched arrow pinned the tongue to the roof of the drooling mouth. Before the creature could react Henri Delacrois loosed a second shaft. And a third. One disappeared into the cavern of the monster's mouth. The other shattered on the scales surrounding the lips. Snatching another arrow from his quiver Henri aimed for the tongue before the thing could work the first shaft free.

Ralf unlimbered his battle ax as two sailors snatched iron tipped spears from the weapons chest lashed below part of the railing. They knew, as all did, that cold iron interfered with many magics. But not this time. Their thrusts and slashing cuts to the scaled belly produced only bright sparks.

Then Ralf heard his name called above the noise of battle. He turned to see Tishimi Osara urgently beckoning to him. He dodged around Henri as his comrade loosed yet another shaft. Behind the mast Tishimi waited impatiently, her foot on the loop of the vertical line up the mast.

"Get me to the top," she said her voice calm amid the chaos. As Ralf grabbed the coil of rope she drew her katana.

Ralf rammed his arm through the coil. The hemp bit into his bicep. Ducking under the lower yard of the sail he hurried forward. Dodging eyebolts, chests, and other obstacles on the ship's deck he almost trotted after the wisp of a woman's weight came on the line. Soon he could go no farther forward. He turned to begin pulling the rope hand over hand at almost the same speed.

Then the rope stopped dead. Ralf gasped. He invoked the name of Thor that the line had not snagged. Then he saw Tishimi's head above the sail. Her black silks flickered in the light as she sprang onto the heavy wood cross yard. For a fleeting moment she hesitated as she fought for balance. Then she fairly bounded to the end of the beam. Firmly balanced again, she looked down as the Stoorworm bellowed with pain. Then the Bournemouth tore the forked tongue free from the roof of its mouth.

Before the creature could move closer to the castaway Henri put a shaft into one of its eyes. The monster reared up twisting backward. Tishimi dived off the yard katana extended.

Ralf's eyes almost left their sockets as the tiny woman, blade in a two handed downward grip, landed on the Stoorworm's back. Her sword sank deeply into the body, bisecting a scale as it did. Now Tishimi grabbed one of the protruding neck ridges with one hand. She rammed one of her bare feet into a gap between two other ridges. Using her other leg as leverage she tore the katana out of the body.

"Henri, stop!" bellowed Ralf as he saw an arrow pass between Tishimi and himself.

Now she began working her way up the spine as the Stoorworm writhed in pain. Ralf could see blood flow as the ridges dug into her feet. But Tishimi continued.

Finally she jammed her feet into two of the ridge gaps. And when the monster's wild undulations brought her upright she struck.

The Katana flashed down between her legs to half sever the creature's body. Blood and other fluids sprayed everywhere as the dying monster began to slide back into the sea. Ralf saw Sinbad grab a line and leap onto the thing. Somehow he climbed up to yank Tishimi's feet free. She kept her blade under control as the Captain guided her back to the deck.

"Stoorworm!"

As the word left his lips the castaway felt his last bit of energy flow from his body. He collapsed on his side. Almost instantly one of the ship's crew tried to pull him further from the rail. Just inside his range of vision he saw hands release the slipknots holding a heavy oilskin on a chest. The cover flew open. Then those hands snatched a bow and large quiver of arrows from inside. In less time that it takes to tell the man with the drooping brown mustache strung the bow. As he threw the quiver over his shoulder he extracted three arrows. Henri held two in his teeth as he nocked and let the third fly.

The castaway watched a blisteringly fast stream of shafts hold the Stoorworm momentarily at bay, but not even the massive Viking could do any damage with a huge ax much less the spears some others used. Then he saw movement along the top spar of the sail. He watched the almost frail looking figure in shiny black disappear on the back side of the monster. Probably glanced off into the sea, he thought grimly.

Barely an instant later the Stoorworm reared up and began to buck like an unbroken horse. Then the head, and about nine cubits of the body sagged forward. The fire of the creature's remaining eye disappeared like a candle thrown into water. The ship's railing splintered as more of the thing's weight came on it. The shards of the railing began to strip off the heavy scales. They rained down on the deck. One of them glanced off his arm to draw blood.

The trunk of the worm's body began to rotate. Now he saw where the sword had cleaved the thick body almost in half. But the one in black's feet seemed trapped.

Bare feet and legs landed in front of him. The Captain! Now Sinbad freed the bottom of the line to the top sail spar from the ring-bolt on the deck. Carrying the line Sinbad sprang to the descending spine ridges of the monster. Like a spider on a dry wall he swarmed up to the one with the strange sword.

The wind freshened. It blew the black fabric tight against the figure as Sinbad tried to release those feet. Only then did the castaway realize the Stoorworm died at the hands of a woman.

"Captain," called the archer pointing to his midsection.

Sinbad glanced in his direction. He nodded. The archer pulled a small ax from his belt and threw it. The weapon arrived with the blade facing back to the ship. The Captain caught and reversed it in a heartbeat. He began hacking at the spine ridges as the creature continued to slide into the water.

Still two body lengths above the deck one ridge shattered. Now Sinbad reversed the ax to smash at the ridge gripping the other foot. Pieces flew in all directions. Sinbad flipped the ax to land blade up on the Blue Nymph's deck. At the same time he took a tighter grip on the woman and pushed away from the monster.

Sinbad's feet barely cleared the rail. Willing hands guided him to a steady landing and relieved him of his burden. The castaway caught just a glimpse of the pain racked face with strangely shaped eyes as he finally passed out.

Slowly his mind came back into the world of the living. His ears heard the groaning of wood and splashing of water. His nose further assured him of being below deck on a ship. He lay on his side on some sort of pad, his back resting against the hull. He shifted slightly assuring himself that his burden remained where it had been. Finally he opened his eyes.

And looked into the face that had haunted his exhausted dreams. Her lips twitched in the briefest of smiles. He wondered what languages she

Sinbad's feet barely cleared the rail.

might speak. Some I've probably never heard of, he thought. The Captain spoke Latin, as did many travelers in Christian lands. He decided to try that.

"I owe you my life. Thank you."

Her eyebrows moved toward each other as she concentrated. Minor errors came with the words as she replied. "No one deserves to be the meal of a serpent. You are welcome."

"I have never seen a woman, or a man, who looks as you do. Your face is strikingly attractive. I hope that does not offend you."

"I am not here to be courted. I am a free woman!"

"Of course. But can not a man admire, without desire?"

"Few that I have met have that ability," she replied. "Here, let me get some liquid into you."

"But your feet..."

"The soles are fine. Omar, that's the Mate, has got the cuts slathered with something to keep infection away. Now pull up the beer through this reed."

A few minutes later he spoke again, "Thank you. May I ask where you have come from?"

"You've heard of Chin, Cathay, China?"

"Yes, but half the stories I do not believe. Supposed to be right on the edge of the world."

She actually gave a snort of a laugh at that, "Not the edge of the world. For I come from the ocean beyond that land."

On the deck of the Blue Nymph the crew bustled around. Some cleaned, packed up and stowed the weapons and other property scattered about the deck. Others drew buckets of seawater to clean the decks before the various remains of the Stoorworm could soak in, or dry. The two best carpenters evaluated the damage to the ship. And the cook rebuilt the fire safe platform of bricks and sand so that the long delayed breaking of the fast could begin.

Below deck, in the Captain's cabin, the relieved to be alive Omar became worried again.

"Waagh, Captain! Go back? Is this for our castaway?"

Sinbad smiled a bit as he finished the wrapping of a dry turban. "Yes, my friend, we go back, for him. Our new passenger even said he would try to pay us. But he could make no promise because his hidden valuables might have been discovered in his absence."

"Try to pay!?"

"That's one of the reasons I believe him, Omar. A scoundrel would have *promised* a treasure bigger than that of the Greek Midas. And, you saw his condition. He'd be lucky to last in the sea until the next dawn. But he told me he would have to turn down our offer if we sailed towards the Pillars of Hercules. He would wait for another ship that would take him home."

"Surely, Sinbad, he spent too much time in the sun."

"I don't think so. He is not a Holy Man, but he failed in a sacred duty. He will take any chance to put that failure right. And that monster shows that someone very powerful does not want him to succeed."

"You mean some evil vizier wants whatever he is carrying?" Omar was flabbergasted at Sinbad's matter-of-fact demeanor.

"Correct. And I've decided we are going to aid him." Omar knew his Captain could be the most stubborn sailor on the Seven Seas.

"And what will that scum from the bowels of Hades throw against us next?"

"The evil mage will have less chance to sink us if we get our new friend ashore. And his homeland is about the closest land. Think how many more chances he'll have should we sail for home."

"A point," said the scowling Omar. "But wait! What is his name?"

"I can not tell you my true name. But, please call me Ian. I have borrowed that from a good friend."

"Ian... Ian," Tishimi stumbled a bit over the unfamiliar word. "A nice short name. Since I joined the Blue Nymph I have met so many people with long names. And titles enormous enough to sink a skiff." She paused a moment as an acrid smell wafted into the area. "Finally! The cooking fire is lit. My body longs for nourishment. But you've gone days. I'll get you some, but you need to go easy."

"I know," replied Ian. "And what might it be? On my last ship we seemed to live on salt pork."

Tishimi laughed outright at that. "With the ship's crew largely Sons of the Prophet? There would be mutiny if someone were dumb enough to try and bring the casks aboard. I hope you like pickled sardines."

Sinbad unrolled a chart painted on thin leather. "We came out of Zeebrugge on the Gaul coast yesterday morning. We shot out of the channel between Gaul and Britannia well before nightfall. And we headed west a minimal speed so as not to run aground before dawn. That puts us roughly here. Somewhere near this heavily forested area is where Ian wants to go. Beyond Wareham, but just before Carisbrooke. Come about and head due east for the time being. I'll write about this morning in the journal. Since the Caliph financed this voyage, we might as well provide him with some entertainment to explain our slow return."

Omar headed up on deck muttering something about being entertained at the bottom of the sea.

Ian finished the small portion Tishimi brought for him, washing the formerly dried fish down with more of the strange ale like liquid. His stomach rumbled and he belched loudly. Tishimi managed not to laugh at that.

"I promise your next meal will be bigger," she said with a smile.

"I have never tasted fish quite like that. Why was it yellow?"

"That is a spice called, I think, saffron. Anything it touches turns yellow. It comes from about half way to my home."

"In that case I'll probably never see it again. And so I'll... Hold! What is that low rattling sound?"

With a curse Tishimi Osara snatched up her set of blades from between two wooden crates. Ian could not understand a word as she berated herself for not keeping the weapons in her sash. The katana seemed ready to jump out of its sheath. As she hurried forward to the hatch she heard Ian call out.

"Thank you, for breakfast."

Omar almost jumped out of his skin when Tishimi practically vaulted out of the small nearby hatch. Tightly gripping the handle of her sword she looked first at the decks of the Blue Nymph. Then she began to scan the horizon. Overhead half the blue sky seemed partly obscured by thin clouds that had moved in while the girl had been below deck. And where she still should be.

Then, on the horizon dead ahead, his eyes caught something like a flash. He stared straight in front of the mermaid on the prow. Something flashed again. And yet again. He turned his head to look at Tishimi. Her hand on the sword's grip seemed to be shaking. He swallowed hard as he returned his gaze forward. Another flash.

"Captain!"

Sinbad looked up from the stand where maps could be mounted. He and Ralf worked there with the Viking's magic crystal to confirm the Nymph's course. Omar pointed at Tishimi. Some color drained from the Captain's face as he hurried back toward the tiller.

Now Sinbad, Omar and Tishimi gazed at the horizon. The flashes came faster. And then almost totally black clouds hove into view from below the horizon. Following the sea-monster, one monster of a storm seemed to be headed straight for them.

"We get plenty of warning, Sinbad" observed Omar. "This time."

"That makes no sense, old friend. Ian told me the storm that smashed his ship gave no warning, at all. This nasty looking thing sends us warning from thirty or fifty leagues away. I can hear Tishimi's sword rattle in its scabbard from here. It's like the Imam shouting 'Fire!' from the Minaret of his Mosque."

"Aye, Captain. Yet wizards and mages often use masking spells to hide their works until trouble seems to rise out of the ground at our feet."

"Perhaps this mage is a simple hireling. And his employer does not know enough to ask for such."

"Sometimes I wonder if even the gods know as much as they are supposed to. I'll get the crew positioned, just in case that storm is a diversion."

Omar returned a moment later. "We have land to either side of us. Not close, but not far enough to be ignored."

"And we will not ignore those shores, Omar. The storm appears to be coming from exactly where Ian wants to go; behind the island with an old Roman fort. We cannot steer directly into it. If we run before it we might be safe. But only Poseidon could tell where we'd end up. But Ian needs to get to his destination by solstice. If we run then the plot succeeds.

"Just north, and to the east of us a bit, is what some call Tor Bay. It is our *best* chance to dodge out of the path of a normal storm. That friend of Henri's told me the bay is deep and has few hazards save for the sandy shore. We'll head there. Break out the oars, Omar. We need as much northing as possible before the winds pick up."

"All hands!" bellowed Omar. "To the oars!"

As darkness fell the Blue Nymph reached the somewhat calmer waters of Tor Bay. Now only half the crew toiled at the oars. The other half "rested" keeping the sail trimmed. Even the mighty Ralf dripped sweat as he stowed his oar.

The rising wind pushed the sail even harder. Canted at a huge angle to the ship's centerline the Blue Nymph headed for a point about half a league from the rounded shore. Clinging to the bowsprit the cook heaved a knotted line regularly into the white capped waves.

"No bottom... No Bottom... Quarter of a cable... Quarter of a cable, less three cubits..."

"Ready with the anchor! Lower sail!" shouted Omar. "Let go!"

All heard the heavy rope begin to run out. Following the splash of the anchor itself, the smell of scorched rope fiber drifted back to Sinbad. The prevailing winds from the storm slowly tuned the Blue Nymph around the point of the firmly set anchor. Finally she swung from side to side a bit with her prow facing dead into the storm winds.

Little rain fell as the storm approached the eastern headlands of Tor Bay, but huge bolts of lightening ripped from one part of the cloud mass to another. Then the center of the storm passed the tip of the spit of land forming the bay. A fearsome bolt flashed down to the ground. All on deck saw a huge old tree at the land's end turned to smoking splinters. Seconds later another bolt set brush afire near the shoreline. Then the massive thunderhead seemed to turn in the direction of the Blue Nymph.

"Tishimi!" called Sinbad as he pointed to the center of the anvil cloud. "Is that what you father's sword warns us about?"

"Aye, Captain."

"Can you do anything about it?"

"I pray my father's katana is strong enough, Sinbad," she replied as she trotted toward the ship's prow.

"So pray we all," came the subdued voice of Omar.

The bolts of lightning paused as the core of the thunderhead rolled past the beach at the tip of Tor Bay. Tishimi reached the Blue Nymph's prow. She scrambled up the plain timbers until she reached the ornamental carving of a mermaid. A moment later her legs slipped over the sea creature's shoulders. She undid the sash of silk around her waist. With it she tied herself in place. Then her hands flashed to the hilt of her sword.

The katana left its resting place with a rasp that not even Tishimi heard over the roaring winds. Barely did the blade reach for the sky when a streak from the forge of Vulcan arrowed down towards the ship. Sinbad watched open mouthed as Tishimi twisted the sword in a two handed grip. The hair on his arms stood up as the blinding bolt hit the flat of the blade. And flashed into the water a stone's throw to port, there the water exploded into froth.

Other bolts followed. Rain arrived in near blinding torrents. The waters of Tor Bay heaved like the open ocean. High winds blew straight into the bow of the Blue Nymph. Time and again those hellish discharges flashed away from the ship. Soon most metals on board began to get hot to the touch. Then the thunderbolts ceased.

Rain still splashed down as if thrown from buckets. The winds now came in from the port quarter of the bow.

"Is it over?" breathed Omar.

"I do not think so," Sinbad replied grimly. "The hair on my arms stood up as the lightning first came, before they became soaked. Now I swear the hair on my head is trying to cast off my turban. The heart of the storm has nearly passed us. Perhaps..."

The very sky seemed to burst open with light and sound. Flickers of lightning arced up from the outlaying clouds to the peak of the thunderhead. The whole roiling anvil cloud pulsed with interior light. Now the glow concentrated in the cloud's edge closest to the Blue Nymph. A huge ball of crackling lightning roared down towards the ship.

Tishimi twisted her body towards the port side. The ball of energy struck. Before his eyes overloaded with the brilliant flash Sinbad saw the ball split in twain. Then he saw nothing but spots for some time.

Sinbad fought the urge to rush forward as the rain abated and the winds eased. But, with his vision still covered with spots, he risked injury or even death. He might trip over gear displaced by the storm; or impale himself on broken timber. Perhaps even fall into the sea. Slowly he felt his way ahead. Truly he had no idea if his friend and crew member would be alive, or dead.

No flashes of lightning now came from the storm. All the Blue Nymph's running lamps were out, if not destroyed. He inched his way to the prow as the spots in his vision faded. He heard Omar calling out the names of the crew. And every name was answered. Though four had someone speak for their unconscious or below decks shipmates.

He heard muffled cursing to his left. He could barely make out the small forward hatch there. Then came the sound of a side of meat smashing into a bulkhead. More curses and the sound came again. The hatch ripped out of its battens. The hinge barely held as the hatch rotated to slam back into the deck.

Henri Delacrois climbed onto the deck followed by Ralf Gunarson. Henri held a package wrapped in oilskin. "Permission to start a flame, Captain?" asked the archer.

"Granted," replied Sinbad formally. "Nothing will burn on deck for some time."

Before Sinbad finished speaking Ralf pulled a wax sealed tinderbox out of the package. Seconds later sparks began to fly as flint scraped steel. By the time the tinder in the small box began to burn Henri held a torch ready to be lit. Then one torch lit another until four brought light back to the deck of the Blue Nymph.

The light showed deck to be a mess. Gordian Knots lay where coils of rope once waited for use. Three small crates had been adrift banging everything in sight. Tossed up by the breaking waves dying fish flopped and sprawled everywhere.

Then they raised the torches and moved forward. Bits of broken hardwood railing crunched under Ralf's boots. The others danced around the large splinters in their bare feet. Finally they pushed the darkness far enough back.

Her body slumped towards the port side of the ship. Her visibly shaking arms still fought to keep the katana pointed at the sky. Her head moved from side to side. She spoke in her own tongue. The men knew not the meaning of the words, but some they had heard when all cursed. Sinbad recognized others as being from a prayer she had once shared with him. Sinbad surveyed both sky and the sea before moving forward.

"Tishimi..." he began quietly as he passed his torch to a crewman. "Tishimi, the storm has passed us. The ship is safe for now. Please, let me sheathe your sword and get you down."

Sinbad gestured. Henri and another crewman now held two torches each as Ralf relinquished his. The Captain felt the iron bands of Ralf's hands encircle his ankles. The mighty arms beyond those hands lifted him like he weighed no more than a child's doll.

Gently Sinbad straightened her body. He knew she would never relinquish her blade. He brought the dangling scabbard up to its usual position. He spoke to her in a firm, but unthreatening voice. He put her left hand around the scabbard's top. Then his longer arms guided her sword arm through the motion he witnessed every time danger ended. He lowered the dull side of the katana until the metal brushed the tips of her fingers. She reacted as he hoped. Those fingers guided the tip to the slot in the scabbard. Her right hand brought the blade home. Only then did she collapse.

Sinbad cradled her torso against his chest while he got a good grip on the far sleeve of her silks. With his other hand he worked to release the efficient knot holding her to the mermaid figurehead. Finally Ralf lowered the two of them to the deck where many arms reached to steady them.

"She breathes well," he told his crew as he carried her toward the large aft hatch. "We all owe her much tonight. Probably our very lives."

The man known to the crew of the Blue Nymph as Ian slipped into a fitful sleep as the thunder abated and the ship's movement returned to normal. The creak of the opening hatch to the deck half roused him. Soon the door to his small cubbyhole eased open. A burning splinter of wood relit the small lantern in the space. Ian blinked as even that amount of light blinded him.

Then a man stepped in, blocking most of the light. Ian's eyes recognized the shape of Sinbad's turbaned head and body. But what was that he carried? Then the Captain knelt at the pallet across from the castaway.

Ian sat up in a rush that caused spasms in his muscle knotted torso. "Is she badly injured?" he gasped.

"Her heart beats strongly. She breathes slowly, but deeply," replied Sinbad taking in the genuine concern on Ian's face. "She, along with her father's sword, warded off the many strikes of that devil's storm. We all pray that she is merely exhausted. Perhaps even more than you were yesterday."

Behind the Captain Ian saw Ralf clutch an Icon on his belt as he looked upward. Henri crossed himself.

"Tell me what needs to be done for her," said Ian firmly. "I will take care of her as she did me. Or tell me how else I might be of help to the ship."

"Keep her warm and calm, my friend. The rest of us go to begin repairs. And keep watch. I doubt we've heard the last from those seeking to end your mission."

"I doubt that, as well, Captain Sinbad. May you, the Blue Nymph, and all her crew be blessed for helping me."

Dawn found Sinbad sleeping as only a sailor can when his ship has been damaged, eschewing the comforts of his cabin bed. He dozed fitfully seated on a clear space of the deck, his feet pulled up. His arms rested on his knees. His turban served as a pillow of sorts resting on his arms. His mind ignored the sounds of saws, adzes, and drills as the crew worked to replace damaged wood. Bare feet stopped beside him. He spoke without moving.

"What woe do you bring to me now, Omar?"

"No more than we had when you lay down your head, Captain. But the glass has turned."

Sinbad raised his head to twist out the kinks of his neck. He stretched as he rose saying, "I have the watch. Any news?"

"The crew works well, but I will be glad to have all the torches quenched. Much has dried out, and not even dew as Allah brings on the new day."

"Sleep, if you can, old friend."

As Omar folded himself into a ball on the deck Sinbad once more mused on how fire served as both friend and worst enemy of ships and sailors. Tar and pine pitch protected many parts of a sea going vessel from water leaking. Or from the corrosive actions of the ocean's salt. But that meant the standing rigging ropes that took stress off the mast and even the seams of the decking could catch fire in a heartbeat when dry. Use of fire could only be authorized by the officer of the watch. Sinbad reminded himself to thank Henri for remembering that in last night's aftermath.

Now Sinbad could just see the beach of Tor Bay, about three cables distant. Nothing moved on the shore. He glanced about the deck. Half the crew lay curled up or sprawled for what rest they could get. When the sand glass turned again they would rise to take their turn working.

This time of day the cook should be preparing his galley below deck. But the cook also was the best caulker aboard. He now pounded replacement oakum, mixed with pitch, onto the deck's seams. After an informative turn around the deck Sinbad got to work.

He laid out the required pattern of fire-bricks. Shaking damp sand into the cracks between the bricks he clamped the wide metal bars together to hold them in place. He added sand to the top of the metal. Then Sinbad went below for wood and to look for dry tinder.

Omar awoke with a frightened start as the smell of burning wood infiltrated his nostrils. But, before he finished sitting up, the aroma of the hot

Sinbad could see the beach of Tor Bay.

griddle eased his fear. He found his bare-chested Captain, half his chestnut skin lightened by flour, folding fresh caught fish and sliced yams with a few herbs into sheets of unleavened dough. He then drizzled the packets with olive oil. As the Mate approached Sinbad used the bread paddle to place six portions on the hot griddle.

"Watch and turn those," said Sinbad cheerfully as he began to roll more dough.

"Aye, the crew is hungry enough to eat the scrap wood. But if you don't learn how to handle flour more efficiently you'll be whiter than Ralf or Henri."

Sinbad's bellow of laughter reached clear below decks.

The man calling himself Ian roused at the laughter. Somebody managed to find some cheer, he mused. The Captain? Yes, that had been Sinbad. Then he looked over at Tishimi. Now she lay sprawled on the other pallet in the cubby. Both face and body seemed relaxed.

When Sinbad left her in his care Ian could see knots of muscle beneath her black silks. He moved over to her. A shake of her shoulder produced no response. But he could feel everything bow-string tight beneath his fingers.

She lay on her side like a curled up cat. Careful not to disturb the shielded blades, he began massaging her neck and shoulders. Now, with something worthwhile to do, Ian lost the feeling of uselessness that drained his spirit since coming aboard; useless while others fought to protect him. As his fingers and hands worked to help this miraculous woman, strength flowed back into his very soul.

As he worked the muscles of her sword arm's bicep she woke. Ian knew this when her left hand somehow drew her short sword. The blade stopped a finger-width below and away from his sternum, and stayed there, despite muscle spasms in her arm.

"Be at ease," he whispered in Latin. "I am only working to get the knots out of your muscles. I doubt you could walk now. You have saved my life. For now I am your humble servant. I would never hurt you."

The short sword clattered to the deck. She turned her head to look at him. Tension still distorted her features. "I believe you. I don't know why, but I do," she replied. Her lips tried to smile, but could not. "Please continue, oh humble servant."

Much later he returned to his own pallet. His hands felt ready to fall off. But he slipped into a dreamless sleep in seconds only to rouse at Sinbad's guffaw.

A good meal under his belt, Ian stood between Sinbad and Omar studying the leather chart.

"...and, after we pass Wareham, can we safely sail behind this island of the Roman fort?" asked Sinbad.

"I see no reason not," replied Ian. "I've seen much larger ships than the Blue Nymph go through. Some even anchor in that small inlet. They climb up to Carisbrooke looking for supposed Roman treasure. And return with nothing but sunburn and insect bites."

"Isn't that the way most treasure hunts go?" snorted Omar.

"Don't they, indeed," chuckled Sinbad. "Now, here's what I propose we do. Skirt the north side of the channel as closely as is safe with the skiff tied along that side. Ralf, Henri, Tishimi and I will be in it with Ian. We will be passing thick forest then. At some well covered point, where Tishimi detects no magic, we cast off. We hide the skiff and head inland. Ian, you did say you know these forests?"

"Indeed. And much of the shoreline, too. We will have to stay in forest, for the roads are too well traveled. And the good folk do like to talk. A day or so of careful walking will get us where I need to go."

"Excellent, my friend," replied Sinbad. "Omar, you take the ship clear round the island. Should you meet locals try to barter for some cargo. The Nymph is looking to take back strange things not found in our home port. Strike any reasonable bargain. Word of that will spread. Keep circling the island, or perhaps put into Portchester, until we signal to be picked up."

Omar snorted. Just as Sinbad headed below he asked, "Think you there's a cargo here worthy of your fancy clothes?"

"Fancy clothes?" said Ian.

"Aye," replied Omar. "Sinbad keeps a couple changes of very costly raiment. Bright silks. Jewels for the turban. Fancy handled weapons. He wears them to make public reports to the Caliph, or to sell strange cargos to those with wealth. Shore going clothes we call them."

The sun stood high in the sky when Tishimi Osara finally came on deck. The indigo sail provided little shade so awnings flapped in the sea breeze fore and aft. A layer of heavy sailcloth covered the shaded area where she most often meditated and passed the time in the company of her own thoughts. She found Ralf and Henri sitting there working on their weapons.

"Plenty of room for you, Tishimi," grinned Henri with a leering wink. He gestured to the array of sharpening stones and other paraphernalia.

The girl ignored the wink, as she did all his futile and supposedly romantic gestures. She stepped behind Ralf, sat and leaned against the Norseman's broad back.

"Good day, little sister," the Viking said as he flipped his huge sword end for end.

Tishimi drew her short sword as she remembered how she had trouble even picking up Ralf's weapon. She fell to work, first checking the hand grip.

Finally, both of her blades ready for action, Tishimi looked over at the assorted piles of Henri's arrows. Steel tipped, bronze tipped and even flint tipped, but all flew true. The Frank was indeed a master. He sat working beeswax into his spare bowstrings.

"Has Ian drawn a weapon?" she asked.

"Indeed he has," replied Ralf. "The middle sized of the three broadswords Sinbad bartered for in case I ever loose my friend here. He took the feel of all three first. Henri and I saw enough to want to be sure he's on our side."

"Yet he seems so quiet. So gentle. And so sad," observed Tishimi.

"Unlucky at love, unlike me," said Henri with a grin.

"Aye," rumbled Ralf, "be he who I think, very unlucky in love. Ian's told Sinbad his story. But Sinbad promised not to speak of it. So I will not, for now. We trust our Captain. He trusts Ian. That is enough."

"For once, you walking tree trunk, I agree. We trust Sinbad with our lives every day. But you will surely tell us, sometime."

"Indeed, little man. If Sinbad or Ian reveal the secret I will tell all I know. Or, after we pass the Pillars of Hercules, I will spin sagas you will find hard to believe. Among them will be Ian's story."

Two hours later, with the sun well past it's apex in a cloudless sky, the five beached the skiff on a tiny pebbled beach. Hurriedly they hid the small craft behind the trunk and roots of a huge fallen tree. Then they vanished from sight into the thick forest. Out of sight of the shore, and beyond the sounds of the water, the group took stock.

"Ian," asked Sinbad, "do you know our position?"

"Only roughly, Captain. If we go straight north we will reach a road in one to two leagues. That distance will tell me what I need to know. Then we follow the bearing of the road, but well out of its sight. There are a few bogs in the forest. We need to step carefully. Once I know our location we should be able to avoid them.

"Just remember that we may well meet honest and honorable people in this forest. Wood cutters, folks hunting small game, and more. We can't attack them without cause. We need to avoid them, if possible. Tishimi, your help detecting magic will be invaluable. We leave when Captain Sinbad is ready."

"And I am ready now. Ian says that we may hunt when away from any roads. No one will think twice about a small cook fire in daylight. But, our camp will be dark. Lead the way, Ian."

Ian shifted the burden strapped to his back, then quietly stepped toward the north.

The near Solstice sun beat down on the canopy of the forest, but the crowns of the trees were high and thick. The party stayed cool. For eyes used to sun both from above and reflected from the sea, the place seemed gloomy. All remained alert, but those from the Blue Nymph mostly kept company with their own thoughts. Twice the sound of Henri's bowstring broke the silence. Two hares went into the game pouch. All carried leather canteens and blocks of hard, dry bread. Fresh game was very welcome indeed.

Ian forged ahead sure-footedly. About a league later, and just before they reached the road, Sinbad called a brief halt. The mariners all listened to the song of the forest. For there were the sounds of birds, insects and animals new to them. New and different smells, too.

As they rose to continue Ian whispered, "I remember the first time I stopped in this forest. This place shows how great is the Creator."

Sinbad smiled. "For landsmen, I agree. For sea-folk losing sight of all land shows the vastness of his work. However one prays those are lessons well remembered."

About a cable south of the road they walked more than two leagues. Three times they took cover to escape notice when parties of travelers headed to the sea on the road. An outrider for the one large party passed about halfway between them and the road.

Finally they came to the ruins of a large building and its compound. Heavy stone walls still stood, but all combustibles had long since become dust.

"Once this was a fine inn for travelers," Ian commented wistfully. "Then a crew of cutthroat robbers took it over. I was part of the party that cleaned it out. The leader set fire to the place rather than surrender. Perhaps, someday, the inn will be reborn. We turn east here."

East they went until the afternoon was gone. They dined on succulent hare roasted on sticks. As the leftover meat dried over the coals of the fire they chatted. With the meat jerked and the fire out they continued east until dusk. Sinbad arranged watches before they slept.

Came morning the party gnawed on jerked hare and the rock hard bread soaked with water as they began walking. A league or so later they came to a spot where the ground naturally branched in three directions.

"Can you choose for us, Ian?" asked Sinbad.

"Aye, Captain. The right hand will waste much time but eventually goes where we wish. The left is far the shortest. Many think the center goes to a dead end, but those of stout heart can get through. Let us try the left hand one, but be wary."

They continued half a league down that path, then Tishimi spoke up. "There is magic up ahead. I have no way to know if it bodes good or ill, but it is there." The warrior woman offered all the touch of the hilt of her sword.

"In this forest," said Ian, "it might simply be an Arch Druid at worship. Or a wizard ready to strike at us."

"Can we reach the other ways without doubling back?" asked Sinbad.

"The center one, yes. The going will be a bit harder until we reach it."

"Are you up to that, my friend?"

"I will not be as fast as I usually am, but I will make it.

"To the center way, then."

Reaching the center route they rested briefly. Over two leagues further the ground rose in front of them. Another league and the steep sides of hills three times the height of the Blue Nymph's mast almost encircled them, like the Greek letter Omega. Huge trees grew almost to the walls of the enclosed area.

"There is a way through here?" asked Henri.

"See the notch in the wall ahead?" replied Ian. "Two hills form a saddle there. Once past the saddle we will walk downhill until we reach the plain of the main forest again. There is a series of ledges in the hillside to our right, much like a staircase. But they are tall steps indeed. A few of them must come up to Tishimi's chin. With the trees nearly as tall as the hills and set so close in, most people do not notice the Giant's Path, as a few call it."

Some of the steps stood but a single cubit tall. A few were nearly three cubits. Most fell in between. But the distance between the steps never exceeded one. Having been there before Ian led the group. Tishimi stayed with him. Sinbad and the others followed a few ledges behind.

About two thirds of the way up a rumbling broke out above them where the hillside bent back and away. Sinbad saw Ian snatch up Tishimi. He tossed her two ledges further before he scrambled after her. Looking the other way Sinbad saw Henri sail into the nearby trees as a massive rock slide came tumbling down at them. Then gravel and small rocks began to pelt him. An upward glance and Sinbad dived toward the branches of an oak tree.

Cut off from the rest of the party, Tishimi and Ian looked at the ledges below them. They saw the steps clogged with rocks and boulders, but with no immediate sign of their companions..

Quickly, they took stock.

"If this was deliberate," whispered Ian, "we must not let them stay above us."

"Agreed. When there are no enemies we come back."

They finished clambering up the natural giant sized steps to the saddle between the two ridges. The girl surveyed the way ahead. The side walls of the saddle made for slow climbing at best. A long cable ahead of them the land disappeared abruptly. Tishimi shook her head.

"You don't like the lay of this land?" Ian chuckled grimly.

"No," came the reply. "We can't retreat with the way we came blocked.

While there's no cover for a group of archers on the ridges, a hidden lookout or two could keep watch for us. The downturn of the path could hide
anything. In fact..."

The haunting note of a horn split the eerie silence of the saddle.

"What?"

"Hunting horn," breathed Ian. "I imagine we are the hunted. What now?
Giant buzzards? A dragon, perhaps?"

"Ian, there is no mag..."

A loud battle cry broke her word in half. An instant later four men's
heads in helms and metal studded leather armor appeared over the far end
of the saddle. Two steps later their chests rose into view. And the heads of
the next row of warriors. And the next. And the next. The span of a breath
later twenty men sporting a variety of weapons trotted towards them in
formation.

Tishimi grabbed Ian's arm. She pulled him down until they faced eye
to eye.

"Ian," she said firmly, "there is no magic here. No magic at all. Just men."

The man calling himself Ian recoiled. He drew himself to his full height.
In less time than it takes to tell the cloud of uncertainty vanished from his
face. His eyes narrowed as he turned toward the rushing foemen. Then his
face became like granite with determination. Tishimi did not believe the
Latin words that came from between his clenched teeth.

"Just men! Then by all that is Holy I will not be beaten. I cannot be
beaten!"

With that Ian's broadsword fairly sprang from its scabbard. Shouting
fearsome words Tishimi did not recognize the transformed man charged
directly for the heart of the oncoming formation. A prayer on her lips
Tishimi drew both blades to sprint after him.

Sinbad el Ari clung to the branch of a hundreds of years old tree about a
dozen cubits above the ground. His wild dive off the series of ledges carried
him clear of the rockslide. Now he looked around for his men.

The feet sticking outside the boughs of a thick fur tree belonged to Henri. The Gaulish archer fought to bring himself back upright. But the huge
Ralf he could not see. Not in the trees. Not on the ground.

Ribald cursing came from the fir tree. "Henri, quiet!" hissed Sinbad.
"Can you see Ralf?"

"I'll see nothing, Captain, until I get this mess out of my face. That big oaf tossed me here before I could even think about moving."

"Who's an oaf?" came a muffled voice from back on the cliff-side.

At the sound Henri disappeared completely inside the fir boughs. Grunts and short curses marked his descent to the ground. He emerged from under the branches just as Sinbad called out softly.

"Ralf, where are you?"

In answer some rocks clattered down from one of the ledges. As the shipmates watched in astonishment a portion of the rocks piled on that ledge began to move outward. More and more stones, some as big as a man's head, began sliding to the floor of the notch. Henri jumped even further back. Now, from his higher perch, Sinbad could see the Viking's metal clad wooden shield. The shield withdrew only to push out another cascade of debris.

"A chunk of rock fell out of the wall here once," called Ralf's now unobstructed voice. "That and my shield were enough. Now show me the son of Loki that caused this..."

Sinbad chuckled, "We shall endeavor to do so, my friend. But more trouble may lurk here. Henri, did your bow survive?"

"Praise God, it did indeed. Broke the string. But I carry five extras. Arrows are scattered, but mostly whole."

"Good. String up and keep watch. Ralf and I will use the grappling hook to try to clear the way to the top."

Sinbad dropped from branch to branch to ground. He nearly bounced up the waist high ledges until he encountered debris from the rockslide. Using a stick, along with the grapnel he carried, Sinbad swept the lightly covered steps mostly clear. He ascended to the freshly cleared step and repeated the process. By the time he reached Ralf the mighty Viking had cleared the step with the notch that saved him. He now used his shield to work on the next ledge up.

When Sinbad arrived Ralf took the hook and rope. Without a word he cast the grapnel three ledges up where man sized boulders clogged the already tough passage. Henri sprinted for the ledges as those huge rocks bounded down into the notch. The archer joined his shipmates just as the grapnel again flew upward.

The hook again found purchase. Sinbad and Ralf strained to loosen a group of stones jammed hard together. Just before the pile began to move Sinbad heard the twang of a bowstring almost in his ear. A scream began in the tallest branches of one of the forest giants. Before the sounds reached the ground they disappeared under the noise of sliding rocks.

As quiet returned Sinbad inquired, "Any more of them, Henri?"

"I do not think so, Captain. But, perhaps more higher up."

"Agreed. Both of you keep watch. I can clear these last few ledges."

As Sinbad swept the rocks from the last area covered by the slide the hills echoed in all directions with many voices in a strident war cry. A handful of heartbeats later a single bellow answered that cry.

"That's Ian, God help him!"

"Yes, Henri. Hurry men, perhaps *we* can arrive in time to help!" said Sinbad as he began to scramble upward, heedless of the possible danger. The Viking and the Frank kept up as best they could.

The sound of steel upon steel ended just before Ralf and Henri sprinted up the steep incline to the top of the saddle in their Captain's wake. The path twisted a bit near the top, dashing around the bend they nearly smashed into Sinbad. They stepped one to each side of their leader. They froze at the desolate sight.

Death seemed everywhere on the saddle. Many bodies sprawled from the center of the saddle to the side slopes. Stray arms and a head or two punctuated the gristly landscape. Only one small figure, wearing black silks, stood. From behind a hip tall pile of bodies Tishimi nodded at her shipmates as she put away her blades. Then she knelt, almost disappearing from sight.

Sinbad and the others dashed forward. Just past the gruesome stack of dead men they found her cradling Ian's head in her lap. The man gasped for air as if he stood on the highest mountaintop in the world. But there was not a single cut on his body.

"By Thor's hammer," breathed Ralf, "a berserker! A true berserker!"

"No, Ralf," said Tishimi. "I've heard you speak of those mad warriors. Ian did not go mad. Somehow he knew... After I told him there was no magic here, he knew. Said he could not be beaten."

Ralf caught his Captain's eye. Sinbad responded by saying, "Henri, see if you can find some whole spears to make a litter."

With his friend out of earshot Ralf spoke so that only Sinbad could hear him. "There's a legend in these lands, Captain. Of a man who can never be bested in single combat. Others claim odds mean nothing to him, if only he believes. Could this, this Ian...?"

Sinbad held up his hand. "My oath prevents me from speaking about Ian. Make of that what you will, my friend. Now, let us find the rest of a litter, if our friend has not cut all the material to pieces."

Ian's breathing slowly crept back to normal. Tishimi watched as the light of life returned to his half lidded eyes. She stroked his head with the tips of her fingers. Then he turned his head to look up into her face.

"I know you are not here to be courted," Ian whispered, "but a man's dreams could be answered wakening like this. I saw little of you during the fight. I was afraid I might smite you in error."

The girl laughed a little. "I watched your first few strikes before I caught up to you. I did my best to stay both on your blindside and out of your sword's reach. Those trying to come up behind you kept me busy."

She paused, then continued, "You are a man of honor and compassion. I can picture a life with the two of us together. But that can never be."

"Sinbad told me of your debt of blood and honor. I, more than most people, understand the consequences of a forbidden or impossible love. I will not press you, though my heart begs me to."

"That is best, for both of us."

At that point Henri returned with a stack of medium thick wooden spears. Quickly he bound together two clusters of three. Then Sinbad and Ralf trotted up.

"We found their camp just below the saddle," grinned Sinbad. "This leather tent would hold up even Ralf."

The Viking gave an evil chuckle. "And, we shall have ample food and drink. Those who brought it no longer need it. Thank you, Ian, for setting the table."

Two hours later the party reached mostly level ground again. Ralf did not even bother to let go of the rear of the stretcher as they took a quick break. Henri, Sinbad, and even Tishimi had taken turns carrying the front. At the halt Ian protested once again that he could walk.

Ralf made a contemptuous noise, "Even a warrior such as you has limits. You've reached yours, and more. I'd carry you by myself, but this stretcher

...a man's dreams could be answered wakening like this.

is far more comfortable."

Sinbad clapped the huge man on the shoulder. "Ralf is right. You know he is, Ian. You have no reserve at all. Not surprising, given all that's happened to you. I'll wager we will again need your help, in one form or another. You can't be of help if you fall over from weakness. Agreed?"

Ian continued to fume, but in a much more private manner.

About three leagues later they twisted their way through the thick forest of huge trees. Light coming through the leaves and pine needles became an ever changing pattern of small circles on the soft forest floor. Then a patch of light appeared ahead. The trees thinned out as an almost flat outcropping of rock rose above the soil.

"Cross it, or go around it?" asked Henri.

"A little of both," replied Sinbad. "We'll circle just inside the tree line. With all our eyes wide open. Ian, you walk this part."

A golden orb seemed to drop right out of the sun overhead into the clearing. A near perfect sphere, it had about the diameter of a water cask and the reflective surface of glass. A longer shaft of slightly darker golden metal spun with a hissing sound at the device's center while the rest of the thing rotated slowly, as if looking for something.

As one the party form the Blue Nymph guessed who the thing sought. Sinbad signaled for silence, then motioned to take cover. They ducked behind trees as silently as they could. But Ralf's luck did not stay with him.

He stepped almost directly on the nest of a pheasant. The startled bird squawked loudly, then bolted almost directly for the orb. The outer part of the spherical device spun to face the bird, and the party. The movement revealed a multi-facetted green crystal lens. From that seemingly living jewel flew a beam of deep purple.

The pheasant suddenly glowed purple, just before it dropped to the ground like a stone. A second pulse of purple sought Ralf, but the Viking somehow managed to hide his huge body behind the tree trunk next to the bird's nest. A portion of the tree turned purple, but nothing seemed to happen to it.

Henri lobbed a stone toward the thing from well away from where the crystal lens pointed. The orb spun. The stone glinted purple. It dropped straight to the ground an instant later. Now the orb twisted in all directions. Purple bolts flew wildly. The center shaft of the device spun even faster. The orb darted away from the center of the clearing.

The spinning center shaft of the thing glanced off a large tree. The orb changed course like a thrown flat stone skips off of still water. The device bounced off another tree straight towards Tishimi. The warrior woman's katana flashed up as the orb unleashed another purple bolt. The sword fairly sang as it reflected the purple beam, straight into Sinbad.

The purple hit Sinbad squarely in the chest. In less than an instant the Captain's whole body glowed in purple hues. He did not seem to move as the purple moved two hands width away from his body in all directions. A shell seemed to crystalize around him.

"Nooo!" shouted Tishimi as Sinbad began to float upward. Then, with a sharp crack, he disappeared.

Sinbad's feet drifted downward. He could see torches flickering with an unnatural slowness.

He seemed to be surrounded by a wall of warped, but ever changing, glass. Glass with bits of fog clinging to it. Wooden stands he could just make out held sheets of parchment and cured hides put in place with tiny nails. His eyes began to come level with the top lines of writing. The characters looked intriguingly familiar, but he knew them not.

Then the extended tip of his big toe brushed the floor. The misty flexing glass vanished in less than a heartbeat. All the forces of the everyday world suddenly returned to normal. Not being fully upright, Sinbad sprawled to the surface of the place. His turban came down on a rock half the size of a hen's egg. Without the layers of cloth his wits would have left him.

Sinbad lay as if truly stunned. He let his arms move as if he lacked the ability to control them. His legs twitched.

All this assured him that his dagger remained strapped to his calf and the things in his sash were still there. Through slitted eyes the captain of the Blue Nymph accessed the situation.

A dungeon, he thought? No. Little sign of man's work in the structure of the place, except for the wooden door fitted into a existing opening. Part of a natural cavern modified by the hand of man.

He saw no movement. Felt no eyes on him. His scimitar lay to one side. Point and hilt rested on the ground. The blade's razor edge lay against the rough hewn wooden legs of one of the tripod stands holding the strange writing.

Sinbad groaned loudly and rolled over, as if asleep. The view at the back of the cave told him little. A sleeping pallet, long disused, by the look of it. A small stack of papers, a low table on which rested three unlit candles. All very neat and in place.

With still no hint of being watched Sinbad slowly arose. Looking around again he straightened his forest battered clothing. He took one step towards the door. Then he fairly leaped to snatch up his scimitar. Crouched in a fighting stance, he watched.

Nothing happened. He listened with his ear to the door. A sound that might be distant falling water reached his ears. Mixed in came a few noises that did not seem to be of nature's making.

He drew first a small brass mirror, and then a length of flexible bronze wire from his sash. He twisted the wire through two holes in the mirror. He brought the mirror past the edge of the eye height hole in the door. Now he looked out without exposing himself.

A few twists of the mirror showed him he had not needed to bother. Another unoccupied room lay outside. This one held a large table and several chairs. The table and all but two of the chairs sagged under the weight of huge books and all the apparatus of the scientist, or, more likely, the alchemist. A single torch lit the room. But even more light flowed in through the opening into a much larger space.

Sinbad fell quietly to work on the door.

Back at the forest clearing Tishimi cursed in more languages than her companions knew she spoke. Tears ran down her enraged face. She glared at the orb now seemingly fastened in place about the height of the Blue Nymph's mast above the center of the clearing. Low and deadly, her voice reminded Ralf of the frozen solid fjords of his homeland.

"Ralf, stand here. Henri, get on his shoulders. From your shoulders I should be able to throw my katana into the foul thing." Before the others could move, Ian's voice broke in.

"I would not do that. Not just yet, anyway. I do not think the Captain is dead. Or even hurt, yet."

"Why say you this?" demanded Ralf.

"Because of the other results of the purple spell. The tree seems undamaged. The rock Henri threw is not destroyed. Only stopped. And look the pheasant struggles to rise. See! Now it walks. I'll wager anything that the magic was supposed to transport a human somewhere. Only it took the wrong human. Conjurers have told me that many spells can be reversed. If this one can that orb will be needed for the thing to work. I say leave it alone, unless it attacks. I can wait one more day and still complete my mission. I will wait here, and pray for Sinbad."

And so did they all.

Cutting a Lambda shaped notch with his dagger at the join two of the door boards, Sinbad listened intently. No sounds approached. After some effort the notch became an opening about the thickness of two fingernails. This the tip of his scimitar widened. Soon the whole sword blade could reach into the room. The curve of the sword blade allowed him to imbed the point of the blade into the bar across the door. Sinbad lifted. He tried futilely to slide the bar to one side.

Cursing, Sinbad stepped to the rear of the room. He sliced open the sleeping pallet. His nose rebelled as he pulled out the smelly uncured wool stuffing. He lit one of the candles. As the tallow began to melt he cut a triangular length of wood from one of the tripod stands. This he centered on the tip of the scimitar's blade. He dripped tallow over metal and wood to join them. Then he wrapped the tip of the scimitar blade with strands of wool. Still listening impatiently he saturated the whole arrangement with tallow.

Now the scimitar barely fit through the opening. Sinbad brought the padded tip up against the bar. If this didn't work the time for stealth would be at an end. He lowered the sword's hilt to the dusty floor then thrust sharply upward. He felt the bar fly upwards. Before the bar could descend he threw his weight against the door.

The portal opened a good hand's width, then jammed. He removed the sword from the slot to thrust it, and his arm, into the room. A moment later he pushed on the bar from the outside. Removing his weight from the door he flipped the bar fully open.

Sinbad burst through the door ready for an attack. None came. The bar made little noise settling into the wooden channel built to hold it. Now Sinbad headed outside the second chamber.

The narrow natural cavern meandered this way and that. Torches, a few about to burn out, held the eternal darkness at bay. The further from that first room the more the torchlight reflected from the walls. The crystalline sections of those walls reminded Sinbad of the caves near his Moorish mother's home city. And of those on the Isle of Colossa. Both were said to be the retreats of wizards and mages. Perhaps such places are conducive to sorcery, thought Sinbad.

Then the cave branched. One path opened up both in width and height. The noises he heard before came from that direction. But the uneven floor of the smaller branch had been swept recently. Sword in one hand, dagger in the other, Sinbad crept down the smaller passage.

He soon found an opulent bedchamber. Half the oil lamps had gone out, but still the walls glowed brightly. For the walls held far more crystal than anyplace he had seen. Carpets covered the floor. Silks hung from above shimmered in the breeze caused by his entry. Sinbad glanced at the few volumes by the head of the bed. The two he recognized, one of them being in Arabic, contained love poetry. A moment later Sinbad emerged, scimitar still in one hand, his other arm wrapped around a bundle.

Now Sinbad explored the other passage. Soon he reached the opening to a huge cavern lit not with torches, but with the six biggest oil lights the sailor had ever seen. Hugging the entrance wall he beheld a waterfall cascading into an underground lake that could almost hold the Blue Nymph. The outlet of the lake disappeared back underground.

Near each of the huge lamps sat a platform. The one nearest him stood empty. Others held paraphernalia of the sorcerer's trade. Sinbad moved to the side of the nearest lamp. He looked around it. No one in sight, but now he could see a raised platform that overlooked the whole area. Quickly and silently he made his way there.

Slowly he climbed the wooden scaffolding holding up the back side of the platform. Once at the top he peeked over the ornate trim of the thing. There he saw the first sign of life.

A figure in a beautifully embroidered robe sat on a stool facing the waterfall. The mage gazed out over a large circular table. Sinbad could not see the surface of the thing, but he could see the heavy books and scrolls that weighted down smaller tables to either side of the man. Sinbad ducked back as a hand reached to the left hand table. No need. For the man found what he needed by touch.

Sinbad gave thanks for the noise of the waterfall. Close conversation would be difficult here. Hearing footsteps, impossible. With one foot and hand braced Sinbad shook out the bundle made up of the sleeping chamber's mattress cover.

Then he eased himself onto the platform. Keeping low with his feet set

Sinbad used a sidearm motion to throw the thick cover as he would a fish-net. The only warning to the mage came when the shadow of the cloth passed over his head. Before he could finish standing Sinbad tackled him. Enveloped in the blinding cloth the fellow quickly felt his wrists pinned down by what must be knees. He opened his mouth only to have the cloth jammed into it. Then he felt something sharp at his throat.

"And now magician," the sailor began, "we will talk about you, and your employer."

Henri Delacrois stood watch halfway through the night when the orb came to life. From barely turning the center shaft sped up until it fairly whistled with speed. The glow of the crystal eye increased as the orb rotated to point the eye straight down. Henri moved to wake his companions. He need not have bothered. All sprang from sleep, weapons at the ready.

Henri grabbed the two special arrows fashioned to fight the thing. Miniature torches ready to be lit by a tiny covered fire. Ian and Ralf would throw small bottles filled with incredibly potent brandy found at the enemy camp. When those smashed on the orb Henri would set the liquor afire.

"Hold," whispered Ian. "The infernal thing does not threaten us."

As he spoke a beam of flickering gold faded into view between orb and ground. Bits of dust in the air and flying insects began to take on a dazzling golden glow.

"By the eye of Odin," rumbled Ralf, "the fog takes form."

Every insect and bit of dust in the pulsing gold moved away from the center of the beam. Seconds later the clearly defined empty space flickered again and again. Now a force threw the dust motes and insects clear out of the beam as the inner shape began to thicken. And thicken yet more.

Tishimi clapped a hand over her mouth to stop a cry of joy. For a shape within the first shape quickly took the form of Sinbad.

Then the beam faded away as the first shape became visibly denser. The thing began to drift downward. Sinbad did not seem to be moving. Then Henri realized the captain had blinked. But that blink took the space of a long breath.

The enchanted vessel reached the sheet of rock that created the clearing. And sank through it. A moment later the toe of Sinbad's boot touched the rock. Before any of those waiting could think, much less act, the shimmering shell vanished completely.

Sinbad reacted barely in time to prevent another fall. Once steady he hurried into the trees. Now the orb righted itself. The crystal lens turned away from them. With a small, sharp boom the orb disappeared.

Tishimi nearly knocked Ralf down as she raced up to Sinbad. "Captain... Sinbad, I am so sorry for what happened," she began.

Sinbad chuckled, "Do not be sorry, my friend. The fates stood with us, this time. I will explain later.

"Ian, we must leave this place now. Trouble may come here sooner, rather than later. Is there a safe way to travel?"

"Aye, Sinbad. There is a small stream bed north of here. This time of year it is normally dry. The stream twists, but mostly in the directions we want to go. But we will walk an extra league for every three or four we could walk in daylight. Is that acceptable?"

"Yes! Far better than dodging that orb, or worse, if we don't disappear."

They found the stream bed half a league north. Finally, as the sky glowed with the false dawn some call the Belt of Venus, Sinbad ordered a halt. With the others staring at him Sinbad began his tale.

"...then I had him. The best way to subdue most practitioners of magic is to bind their hands and prevent them from seeing or speaking. That way they can't make mystic gestures, or shove a knife in your back. And most incantations require speech. Once I got the cloth over him he was done. And he quickly discovered I could slit his throat if I didn't like what he said. So he answered my questions. He spoke a little Arabic, but again Latin was the language we ended up using.

"As Omar and I suspected, the magic trying to stop Ian was hired for the job. By then I realized I was questioning not a white bearded mage, but a relatively young man. The wizard's apprentice, as it turned out.

"Ian, the day before your ship sank, Nabil, the wizard, received a message of some kind. Somebody wanted to hire him. Eli, the apprentice, did not know how, but the pact was made. Eli helped with the sorcery that wrecked your ship. When you survived they took turns watching you in the water for the one who hired them wanted your death to look natural. They even conjured up fog to hide you from passing ships. But you hung on.

"The day before the Blue Nymph found you, Nabil received an urgent summons to a conclave of his entire order. He left Eli to watch saying you were sure to sink soon. Half a day later Eli fell asleep. He woke to find the Blue Nymph coming along side of the mast you clung to.

"Eli threw everything he was able to conjure against us. All the while sending messages for his master to return. He believed that Nabil should arrive sometime today. I learned two more things from him. First, had Ian's burden come through the portal, a number of Nabil's spells would have been invoked to keep both Ian and the burden asleep until after solstice. The orb showed him that the purple spell missed Tishimi, but not that I had been transported. Second, and more importantly, he believes that Tishimi is a sorceress of a powerful secret sect. Having discovered that, I lied to him like the worst rug merchant you ever met in a bazaar.

"I told him Tishimi understood about snatching things and people through the orb's portal. And if he tried to abduct Ian again, that Tishimi was to go thru instead. In that case her orders were to cut off anything that a man might use to cast spells or for pleasure. That took the stuffing right out of him. So I then convinced him to return me before Tishimi brought the whole rampaging crew to his lair looking for me.

"But now, my friends, we must be off. The Mage Nabil may return at any moment. We must finish Ian's journey before he finds us."

They lay on the crest of a hillside looking down at the junction of three roads. Four soldiers stood beside the road leading between two hills. Two carts were just passing the four when the party from the Blue Nymph first crawled to the crest. Now another farmer's cart and a medium sized wagon drove up and stopped. And more could be seen approaching in the distance.

Two of the soldiers looked the rigs over while the third used his knife to make marks on a large board. Then the senior man spoke to all on the rigs. Everyone below seemed happy as cart and wagon moved ahead.

Ian's whisper reached them all, "Everything looks normal for a solstice observance, Saints be praised. Let us crawl backwards, then head for that draw I pointed out."

A few minutes later they reached the steep stony walls at the end of the draw. Ian turned to them with a solemn expression on his face.

"Sorry to say this, my friends, but I must have your vows never to talk about this place. Even among yourselves."

When all had pledged Ian continued.

"I swear in return that, if my quest could be told, I would take you where I go as the heroes you truly are. But that is impossible. None can know how close disaster came. So I must give you my thanks now. Besides you, Sinbad, I give thanks to your Caliph. For had he not sent you to these waters... You may put on your shore going raiment and tell his court our story. Just change, if you please, the location by a hundred leagues or so.

"Ralf, rarely have I called a Norseman friend, but you certainly are my friend now. You as well, Henri. Your fine aim has protected me, and even fed me. Now, if you two would raise up yonder stone and bring me the blue bag that sits beneath it..."

As the two turned away Ian grabbed Tishimi's shoulders to snatch her off her feet. Before she could move he lightly kissed here forehead. Then he placed her gently back on her feet before Ralf and Henri could turn back toward them.

"I will miss you most of all, Tishimi." he whispered.

Sinbad bit his tongue as emotions flashed across the warrior woman's face. Finally she looked into Ian's eyes.

In quiet Latin she replied as a single tear rolled down her cheek, "I will miss you too, Ian."

Then Henri and Ralf hurried up with a leather bag dyed royal blue.

"Thank you, my friends," said Ian. Then he then turned to Sinbad. "Captain, here is the payment I said I would try to deliver to you. Do with it as you will. I am grateful to be able to give it.

"I must send you away now so that I can open a passageway to where I must return my burden. Once inside I will be well protected, even from magic. By the time you reach the road to the sea the danger should be over."

They left Ian there to begin their trek back to the sea. Soon the others began whispering questions for Sinbad to answer.

"Not until we are a full day out to sea," he finally said. "Then I will tell you what I can."

That brought silence to the party. As they continued now, in that silence, Sinbad thought back on the adventure. What was so important, he wondered, about Ian's burden? How important could a single sword be, even a benignly magic one, to this place called Camelot.

THE END

Up Anchor for Adventure

I encountered stop-motion animation at the very first movie I can remember seeing. I figure I was four when my mother took me to see *The Story of Robin Hood & his Merry Men*. That's Disney's live action version staring Richard Todd and Peter Finch.

No animation there, you say? Quite correctly so. But, I remember my mother seriously fuming when the previews were shown for the re-release of *King Kong*. I guess I didn't have nightmares about giant apes, but I did remember Willis J. O'Brian's special effects.

I've lived in suburbia almost all my life. There never was a movie house I could get to on my own growing up. So no matinees with two features, a cartoon and a serial chapter. The movies I got taken to were mostly westerns and swashbucklers. No monsters. No spacemen, except on radio and later, on TV. And TV monsters tended to be real bargain basement deals. Like Jungle Jim seeing stock footage of rear screened lizards made up as dinosaurs. They looked fake, even to young kids.

But, I did see movie previews on TV. Previews for *Earth VS the Flying Saucers*, and *It Came From Beneath the Sea*. Not to mention *Twenty Million Miles to Earth*. Now, there were monsters and special effects I could believe in.

Then came the ads for *The Seventh Voyage of Sinbad*. Somehow I managed to get my folks to take me to it. At the time I did not know that all the movies I've mentioned here helped create the outstanding experience of the new film. Special effects master Ray Harryhausen learned his trade from Willis O'Brian, then created the stop-motion effects for those other films.

Harryhausen brought seemingly organic special effects to color films at a time when even the seriously made first Godzilla movie obviously featured a man in a rubber suit. As important, he built on O'Brian's techniques to make the creatures blend and interact very well with the flesh and blood cast.

He gave the audience both a sense of wonder and a willingness to believe in the story.

Why else would a bunch of writers, artists, editorial, and production folks jump at the chance to get involved with this project? We loved Harryhausen's Sinbad movies and wished for more. And now, after a fashion, there is more.

With a tip of the hat to Big Ray H., I'm darn glad to be a part of it.

Story Notes:

When I came up with the idea for this voyage of the Blue Nymph I reached out to Airship-27's veritable fountain of information on things concerning the British Isles. That, of course, being Ian (I.A.) Watson. Along with Sinbad and Sherlock, Ian writes Airship-27's enthusiastically received Robin Hood novels. (Of course living only a relatively short distance from Sherwood and Nottingham helps.)

I asked Ian for the location of a certain place, preferably not all that far from salt water. As is typical for him, Ian mentioned a number of possible locations. For the one he favored he included a scan of a map with only ancient names on it. Then he appended a long list of Celtic monsters and things that go bump in the night. Everything I needed. And more!

I sent Ian a thank you email and got to work. I put the Celtic sea serpent, the Stroorworm, to work. Those creatures can get as long as a football field, so the thing rising out of the water as high as the Blue Nymph's sail seemed easy. Too bad all that Sushi ended up back in the drink.

A week or so later I decided to find out just where the historical Roman Fort stood on a modern map. And I got a personal shock. That fort was established on what today is called the Isle of Wight. Seems the Ruffin side of my family came to the New World from the Isle of Wight. Here I'd had the Blue Nymph circling one of my ancestral homes and not known it. Wow!

Thanks, Ian. And now you know why the castaway in my tale goes by the name of Ian.

ERWIN K. ROBERTS - is wondering what direction(s) retirement will take him. He should be recently retired by the time this volume sees print. A Missouri resident nearly all his life, he doesn't mind traveling. He still has four, or is it five, states he has not spent any time in. Erwin has been, in no particular order, a cable TV personality, an air-defense missile radar operator, an urban redevelopment business re-locator, and a switchboard operator. He's also worked in a ceramics studio, a truck aftermarket shop, and a couple of graphic arts and sign studios.

He and his wife of over forty years have two adult kids who seem in no hurry to make them grandparents. Lots of money would be nice, but Erwin mostly writes for the love of creating. In addition to his own characters, he really enjoys the chance to write new adventures of characters he enjoyed back in the day. Sinbad now joins the company of the Masked Rider, the Phantom Detective, and a couple of others. Not every one of them is published. The important part was crafting the stories.

SINBAD & THE GOLDEN MASK

By Shelby Vick

"**H**ippocamps don't fly!" First Mate Omar shouted.

"Tell him that!" Sinbad answered sharply, pointing to the monster up in the pale blue sky. Like any hippocamp, its front was that of a horse, this one rust colored, and its rear was that of a giant green-scaled fish – but broad bat-wings spread from its shoulders and where hooves would have been, it sprouted huge scaly claws.

As their ship, the Blue Nymph, sliced through the green-blue water, they watched the thing draw back its wings and dive down. "Strike the sail!" Sinbad ordered.

The sail came down a split second before the hippocamp swooped where it had been. One scaled claw of the hippocamp lashed out and snagged a crewman, who screamed.

Tishimi, whipcord muscled but slim, slashed her magic sword at the fearsome beast as it flew by, but she was too late. Henri was an expert archer, but he feared harming the captured man so he watched as the hippocamp soared into the sky. Blood squirted from the captive as a claw pierced his chest. With a shrilling neigh, the hippocamp dropped the man into the sea far below.

When the corpse hit, water sprayed up, white foam mixed with blue and green, and then something huge rose from the sea and grabbed the unfortunate crewman's body. The scarlet of blood stained the water.

"A kraken!" Tishimi yelled.

"Worry about the hippocamp for now," Sinbad said, lips tightened above his Van Dyke beard. "It's coming back!"

Henri identified three of the crewmen. "You use your bows with skill," he said. "Get them now!"

As the hippocamp turned back toward the Blue Nymph, four bowmen were waiting. "Easy…" Henri murmured as the beast plunged at them, "…easy…Now!"

Bowstrings thrummed. Arrows flew. The hippocamp, however, pulled up at the last moment and only Henri's arrow found a mark, the heavy scales on the hippocamp's claws.

Henri cursed as the monster flew away. "It knows the danger of arrows," he said.

"It's coming back!" Omar shouted.

"Wings!" Sinbad snapped. "Aim for its wings! They are the most vulnerable."

"You two fire first!" Henri ordered, indicating a couple of his bowmen. To the other he said, "The instant they pluck their strings, aim above them!"

Two sets of strings went off a split second apart. The first two arrows flew harmlessly by the hippocamp, but the next two tore through the wings.

With a shrill scream, the monster dropped. Before it even hit the water, the kraken reached up and snatched it into the sea. Water boiled furiously as they sank into the roiled ocean.

Henri glowered and looked at Tishimi. "Those damned scales! No arrow made could go through them."

Tishimi fondled her blade. "It isn't a matter of how sharp the arrows are," she said. "You would have needed magic to penetrate those scales."

Beside them, a large orange tabby tom cat came out of the hold, a dead rat in his mouth. He padded down the deck and, when he was certain his accomplishment had been noted, he began to eat.

"Sail up!" Sinbad yelled. "Zephyr is favoring us, and we need to get beyond this evil place!" In seconds, his trained crew had the blue sail unfurled and, as it caught the breeze, Sinbad reflected on how he came here.

Sinbad had been in port, alone at night, scimitar strapped to his bronze back, a breeze whipping his pantaloons about his brown legs. A robed figure appeared in front of him and gestured for his attention. A glimpse of a woman's face was under the hood of the robe, and her eyes indicated for Sinbad to follow her. With a lack of his usual caution, he went after her into an inn and went with her through the smoky room to a table in the shadowy back. Sudden silence hushed the place and Sinbad noted that smoke rising from a fat man's cheroot has ceased motion and no longer rose.

The woman pushed back her hood, revealing a beautiful and majestic face, the face of Persephone! "I have a task for you, Sinbad," she stated with silky and regal confidence. "I am aware of your travels and your courage and you are the only human I would trust for this task."

Sinbad had learned, long ago, that listening could be more important than talking. Even in the presence of this great goddess, Queen of the Underworld, he retained that lesson, so he just nodded.

Persephone sniffed the surrounding aroma; alcoholic fumes, smoke, the dry hint of sawdust. "Disgusting!" she proclaimed and then uttered a word Sinbad failed to understand. Instantly the scent of fresh air enclosed them, air with the scent of new-mown hay. She nodded with satisfaction, smiled, and continued.

"I can't let the others know I'm involved," Persephone said. "I can be of little help to you. You see, I have been in charge of the Mask of Adonis since it was first created. Unbelievably, some mortal stole it!" She glanced away, and then looked back at Sinbad, admiring his broad shoulders and roguish handsomeness emphasized by a van Dyke beard and meticulous moustache. "I know it was a mortal, as there would have been a trace left by any god or goddess, and there was no trace." Her eyes narrowed. "I must have it back, Sinbad! If you succeed, you will be richly rewarded." She paused. "If you don't succeed," she added grimly, "there is a special place in Hades reserved for you."

Sinbad leaned back and smiled. "There is a saying about being between Scylla and Charybdis, a rock and a hard place, and so on. You wish me to do you a favor, but you tell me there will, literally, be Hell to pay if I fail. Lady, you would never make it in the world of barter."

Surprisingly, a smile crossed Persephone's face. "You, a mortal, would bargain with the Queen of the Underworld? That verifies the faith I have in you, Sinbad. Very well, there will be no penalty for your failure." The smile disappeared as quickly as it had arisen. "The hounds of Hell will not be nipping at your heels, but the Queen of the Underworld will not be pleased with failure." Then she added, "If, no, *when* you find it, you must beware its temptation. It will be in a black silk bag and you must remove it to be certain it is authentic, but then there will be a strong desire to put it on. The desire to wear it will be powerful, but you must not do so! If you do, it will overpower you and you will be trapped forever. Remember my warning!" she said.

"I gather you can give me little help," Sinbad commented. It was a question phrased as a statement.

"The other gods must not know," Persephone agreed. "My help will be… minimal." She made a gesture and knowledge filled his mind. "Now you have the information I have as to the location of the mask. When will you debark?"

A grin split Sinbad's coffee-colored face. A glint of impishness lit his dark blue eyes. "That brings up one immediate way you can help," he said. "A trip such as that requires supplies. I know that you can help me there."

Persephone reached into her robe and brought out a green cloth bag, tied with a gold string. "That should easily handle all supplies," she said. Then Persephone reached into the folds of her gown and withdrew an exquisite dagger. It had a jeweled handle and a slim six-inch blade that seemed to capture the light.

"Sinbad, meet Grachene. He was created by Hephaestus, the blacksmith god. The old cripple," she added with an air of fondness, "did not tell me the origin of the name, only that Grachene loves the excitement of a battle for its holder's life."

"You imply the dagger Grachene can talk."

Persephone smiled. "Only to Hephaestus. As his holder, you may feel an occasional emotion, but that is all." She handed the dagger to Sinbad. "Grachene is unbreakable, and can penetrate anything. I must warn you," she went on, "that Grachene is picky and demands action. He is pledged to you for this task, but after all is over, you may reach for him and he will not be there."

"That could be awkward," Sinbad commented. "I wouldn't care to reach for a weapon and find it wasn't there."

The goddess laughed. "Be not disturbed," she said. "Grachene's absence will come to your mind."

She rose gracefully. "Now, our agreement is met." She waved one hand and Sinbad awoke in the hammock in his cabin on the Blue Nymph as daylight washed across the bay. The green bag was tightly clasped in his hand and he felt Grachene in his sash. "It was no dream," he whispered to himself.

Getting out of the hammock, he went to his basin and washed his face with cold water. "You're committed to this," he told himself. "More, you've committed your crew as well. They shouldn't suffer because of my decision. All gods hear this: I will do my best, but I want to protect my crew!"

Smelling bacon frying, Sinbad went to the ship's small kitchen to see Omar at the little stove. "Feel up to fixing two breakfasts, Omar?" he asked.

Omar turned his square and bearded face to his captain. "Aye aye, sir," he said with a smile. Then his eyes narrowed. "Something has happened," he observed.

"I spoke with someone nameless of great power," Sinbad said. He dangled the bag of coins between them. "We have a task to perform, and will be well paid for it."

Above his grey beard, Omar's lips tightened. "Someone of great power who is nameless because the name of a god cannot be tossed around carelessly," he anticipated.

Sinbad nodded, his own lips tight. "But this person can do little to help us, Omar," he said. "Except for this purse, we are fairly well on our own."

"Curses on Allah," Omar said. A small man, Omar was solidly built; years in his forties, as revealed by the grayness of his hair and beard. Then the corners of his mouth curved upward. "Still, aren't we always on our own?" he added with stoic humor.

Sinbad chuckled. "Quite true." He handed the cloth bag to his First Mate. "Take this and go buy sufficient supplies for a long trip."

A female voice said from behind him, "A long trip?" Tishimi Osara asked. A smile lit her oriental face. "At least it won't be on an empty stomach."

Sinbad was quite familiar with the lovely Tishimi's history. Her father, Tokami Osara, was one of the greatest sword-makers in Japan. Even as a child, Tishimi had shown a great affinity for both weapons and fighting. Since she was a female, her father taught her in secret to master the katana and the short sword until she was the equal of the best samurai.

One day a mighty Warlord came to order a blade. Seeing Tishimi, he later returned with warriors and told Tokami he wanted Tishimi for his concubine. Using the blade he had created for the Warlord, Tokami fought them all and succeeded but was mortally wounded. Tishimi returned to find her father bleeding to death. He told Tishimi to wash the blade in his own blood, and he died.

His blood endowed the sword with magic.

Sinbad's youthful days had been very different from those of Tishimi. He had lived in luxury. His father was a black Nubian prince and his mother a Moorish princess. Sinbad had enjoyed the easy life. At his majority, when he inherited much of the family wealth, he drank away what he didn't waste on women who were attracted to his dark good looks.

Too proud to return home for assistance, he became a Sindhi sailor and learned the ways of the sea as well as how to fight. He learned foreign languages as easily as he had spent money.

"Will this trip involve fighting?" Tishimi asked, hopefulness glinting in her green eyes.

"When has it not?" Omar snorted.

Omar went to the marketplace for supplies, the coin bag tied to his belt. As he walked up, three unruly young men moved to block his way. The tallest, a red-haired man Omar thought of as a wharf rat, said with insolence, "What have we here, an old man going shopping?"

Without pausing, Omar shot out a gnarled fist that hit the redhead in the face, and then kicked him so that he fell back among his cohorts. All three collapsed on the cobblestoned street, and Omar continued forward.

He wasn't followed.

A whisper ghosted through the marketplace and some smiled, others decided they were needed in another place, and merchants greeted Omar with respect. One whispered a secret to Omar, who nodded his thanks.

It was a very large marketplace. Brightly colored silks flapped from wooden staffs. Equally brilliant awnings with tassels dangling from their edges shaded potential customers. There were many booths selling everything from silks to food to ship equipment. "Look at this, good sir!" "Everything one may need!" "The best varieties in the world!"

Stopping at a rope merchant, Omar purchased two large spools of rope. He handed the merchant two gold coins, which the plump man examined. "Strange," he said. "There is no face on these coins."

"Does a face affect the value?" Omar asked. He wondered if the immortal who had supplied the money had done some trickery.

Putting a coin to his mouth, the man bit down. "It seems true gold," he declared. "Just a moment." He reached under the counter and came up with a balancing scale. He put a marked piece of metal on one pan and the coin on the other. Holding the scale by a cord, he lifted it and observed what happened. "Very healthy gold at that," he announced. "Yes, I will be glad to take your coins, face or not." He indicated a large tent behind him. "Our supply of rope is stored there. I will see that yours is delivered."

The First Mate shifted his attention to a clearing inside the market where goat-pulled carts were displayed. "A moment," he said, and walked to the carts and wagons.

A tall and slender man wearing Oriental robes came forth. "The best carts and wagons you may need, sirrah," he said.

"Drivers?" Omar asked.

"Indeed." The merchant lifted one hand. A skinny young man came forth.

"Anyone stronger?" asked the First Mate. "I will have a large load, and it will need guarding."

"Lanir!" the Oriental man called. A bare-chested young man came out of a tent. He had black hair, tanned skin, and a dagger at the belt holding up leather pants. "This man needs our help," the merchant said. He looked back at the First Mate. "Will Lanir satisfy you? His services will add one of your gold coins to the fee."

With trained eyes, Omar watched Lanir approach. He moved smoothly, well-balanced and alert. The First Mate nodded. "Satisfactory," he said. Then, as Lanir led the wagon Omar chose to the rope man's booth, Omar said, "If we return to my ship with everything I purchase, there will be an extra gold coin for you."

Lanir nodded his acceptance.

"Load my two spools of rope on this wagon," the First Mate told the rope man.

The man gave Omar a blank look. "Two spools of rope?" he queried.

Omar leveled his gaze on the man. "The rope I just purchased," he said, with forceful precision. Omar's hand rested on the hilt of his sword. "I am certain you recall that." Lanir moved up beside him, hand on his dagger.

Trying to smile, the dealer backed up and displayed his hands, palms up in submission. "Gentlemen, gentlemen," he said. "Can you not take a small joke?"

'Not when it is about money," Omar said flatly. "Bring out my rope and place it on my wagon."

One spool contained massive hawser rope, while the other was rolled with sail rope.

When it was loaded, Omar stopped at one booth that was displaying a large ceramic jug on the counter. Noting his attention, the owner of the booth came forward. "No ship should be without this!" he proclaimed, placing a long-fingered hand atop the jug. "Its contents help control sea-sickness and, on long trips, prevent scurvy." He put a small cup under a drinking spout at the bottom of the jug. He turned a knob and liquid splashed into the cup, which he handed to Omar. "Take a sip."

The liquid was pale green and Omar's nose reported the scent of citrus. He took a sip and his eyebrows lifted. "It is rather cool," he remarked.

"Yes," said the merchant, pleased. "These jugs are thick, holding back the day's heat."

"Interesting," Omar admitted. "However, our crew consists of experienced seamen, who have no problems with sea-sickness. Further, we are not away from ports long enough to be concerned with scurvy. But thank you for showing me."

The man was disappointed, but accepted the First Mate's decision.

As he added more purchases, Omar noted that the small purse had not decreased in weight. A generous goddess, he thought gratefully.

As they moved along the colorful booths, the First Mate noticed a skinny youngster slipping along behind them, trying to remain inconspicuous. He looked about ten years old and had a filthy white toga over one thin shoulder. In the distance stood a sturdy man with a clean toga and a yellow turban who seemed interested in the young one's movements.

Omar acted as if he had seen nothing until once when Lanir was guiding the wagon past some minor holes in the cobblestoned street. Always observant, the First Mate's right hand snaked out behind him just in time to clasp two thin wrists.

The boy squealed like a startled pig.

Omar lifted him up and held him dangling in front of his grey beard. He studied the trembling child. "Do you ever eat?" he asked.

The surprised boy sniffed and murmured, "Some…sometimes."

Turning his back on the yellow-turbaned man, the First Mate slipped a gold coin out of his purse and put it in the young, bony hand. "Take this to your owner," he instructed. "Tell him there is more on our boat, the Blue Nymph. It is docked at the main port. After giving him the coin, go to the Blue Nymph and tell them Omar said to feed you. Understand?"

There was awe in the response. "That is Sinbad's ship!"

"Quite so," Omar admitted. "What are you to tell them?"

The child licked his lips. "That Omar said to feed me."

"Exactly! Go!"

It only took seconds for the youngster to reach the one he was working for and hand him the coin. "Stop, thief!" the First Mate shouted.

Three guards, hair coiled on their heads, appeared almost magically and started after the boy. "Not the lad!" Omar ordered. "The one with the yellow turban!"

The First Mate's keen eye noted the man's hand going to his mouth as the guards stopped and grabbed him. As Omar neared, one guard asked, "This one, sirrah?"

Omar nodded, and one hand lashed out to the back of the man's head, then slapped forward. The gold coin popped out. Picking it up, Omar said, "This is mine. Take him away and do whatever it is you do to thieves." When he returned the coin to the bag, Omar was certain he heard the approving chuckle of an unnamed goddess.

When Omar was through, there was a large stack of supplies to be dealt with. Omar supervised the loading. Some of the supplies were in boxes, and he bought heavy packing blankets to be wrapped over then for protection during the transit. Then an orange tabby cat dashed after something small and grey which darted under a blanket.

Omar watched as the tabby pulled a blanket back quickly, as if it was only a sheet. Then the cat dove in and, in seconds, came back out with a dead rat clasped in his jaws. With pride, he dropped the rat at Omar's feet.

"Very good," Omar said, smiling. "Are there any more?"

As if fully understanding, the cat began a search of the supplies and eventually had a pile of three rats at the First Mate's feet. Omar stroked the cat's head, then picked it up and cradled it in his arms. "Our ship needs a good mouser," the First Mate said. "After the way you handled that blanket, I dub thee Samson."

The tabby purred.

Omar returned to the Blue Nymph with a bargain in supplies and a talented ship's cat.

As they neared the Blue Nymph, the youngster in the filthy toga stepped out from behind a cluster of roped pilings. Only the toga wasn't filthy this time; it was clean, but wet. "I wanted to thank you, sirrah," he said. "I am filled, and a lady washed my toga. I feel very different now."

Omar beamed down at him. He sensed a change, a strength he had earlier only glimpsed. "You are different, young man. But," he added, "I fear you have no place to go."

"I will return to Samothrace," he was told. "My name is Tros, and I am certain you will hear more of me."

Before departure, Sinbad called his crew together on the deck of the Blue Nymph. They all wore the red vests, leather pants, and gold turbans Omar had purchased. He explained he had gotten the clothes so they would be easily identifiable in a fight with other groups. "As you can tell from the amount of supplies we just loaded," Sinbad told the sailors, "we are in for a long trip. At the very least there will be the dangers of weather, but I feel there will be much more as well. As always, whatever reward we receive will be split amongst the crew. Still, let it be known there will be no shame cast on those who do not wish to face such unknown threats. You will be left at this port, with sufficient gold to support you until you find another opportunity. Do any wish to disembark?"

Ralf Gunarson, the young Viking giant, roared: "What! And miss ad-

"I dub thee Samson."

venture? Not this one!"

One sailor made bold to declare, "You can say that from your great height, Viking, but not all of us have your advantage!" Ralf was at least six feet seven inches in height. His blond hair was braided and his beard was long and yellow. He was wearing leather pants, vest and boots. There was a gleam of excitement in his blue eyes.

Sinbad laughed and held up a restraining hand. "There will be adventure, Ralf Gunarson; no doubt of that. Still, we hold nothing against those with lesser size." His gaze drifted over the assembly of sailors. "Any who wish to remain in port may freely do so. Now is the time, as we are about to sail."

Some crew members exchanged glances, but no one stepped forward.

"Very well," Sinbad said with satisfaction. "The Blue Nymph will sail."

The indigo blue sail soon billowed, and the ship moved out of port, led by its mermaid figurehead.

After the encounter with the hippocamp, Sinbad called Omar into his lavish captain's cabin. "See that the dead crewman's family receives twice, no, double that, what would have been his share."

"If we return," Omar said, with unaccustomed gloom. "We are trying to aid a god, and another god doesn't want us to succeed."

Sinbad slapped his knee in anger. "We will succeed!" he said. "Together, we can do it!"

Omar grabbed his square head with both hands and shook it violently. "Out!" he ordered. "Out, unworthy thoughts!" Then he stared at Sinbad, and essayed a weak smile. "Truly, some god must be affecting me. Sinbad, you know that doubts are not my way!"

Nodding, Sinbad said, "We have already seen the power of one god who opposes us," he said. "As yet, I don't know who but his opposition is obvious. There will be more."

"There is one thing I have not mentioned, Sinbad." Omar took a deep breath and then said, "In the market, I picked up a hint that Rial the pirate is cruising these same waters."

"The pirate of Samothrace?" Sinbad asked, lifting his eyebrows.

"The same," Omar said with a nod. "He may be looking for vengeance."

Sinbad grinned fiercely. "We beat him to the Thessalonian treasure ship and gained a fortune for our troubles. He will definitely be after us; I have no doubt of that. Our ship is better than his," Sinbad went on, "and we have a more loyal crew. I have no fear of Rial but it is good to be prepared. Thanks for the information, Omar!"

The First Mate had a secretive smile above his beard. Seeing it, Sinbad asked, "What else, Omar?"

Omar's smile broadened. "A moment," he said, and stepped outside. When he returned, he was holding a flattened ceramic globe. There was a small hole atop the globe. "I spotted these, and thought they might be useful."

Sinbad's eyebrows lifted in curiosity. "What is it?"

"This is a lamp," Omar said. "Put whale oil into it, then a wick, and you can have light in your cabin if you wish to read at night."

"Why should I read at night?" Sinbad asked. "I know you, Omar; you are holding something back. What is it?"

Omar's smile broadened again. "It would make a good weapon, Sinbad! Most lamps were brass, but these are ceramic. Light the wick and throw it onto another ship and it will break and set the ship afire!"

"A good crew could put the fire out before it did much."

"Then we throw several at a time," Omar persisted. "I bought a dozen of these, as well as a large jug of oil."

"How much did they cost?"

"Not much," Omar said. When Sinbad paused, he continued, "Besides, Sinbad; this cloth purse you were given still contains as much gold as it did to start with. Our nameless patron is most generous."

"Ah!" Sinbad murmured. "That is good. Thanks to the goddess."

"There is more, Sinbad. Having the money, I bought the crew that uniform of red vests, gold turbans and leather pants. When we're fighting another group, it will make it easier to see who's on our side."

Before he could continue, it developed that Rial of Samothrace was just ahead.

"Ship ahoy!" sounded young Haroun up in the crow's nest atop the mast.

Sinbad and Omar rushed out of the cabin. "Where away?" Sinbad called to the crewman above.

"Dead ahead, sir!" Haroun responded, pointing with his spyglass.

"Can you identify it?"

The lookout returned the spyglass to his eye and carefully studied his discovery. "It is …black," he said. "Can't tell more than that."

Sinbad's eyes met Omar's. "Rial is known as The Black Pirate," he muttered. "A black ship can more easily slip up on its target at night."

Omar nodded with bleak anticipation, and then smiled. "We have beaten him before."

"Yes we have," Sinbad mused. He felt Grachene vibrate in warm anticipation of a fight.

Omar knew his captain, and realized his mind was churning. This was verified when Sinbad continued, "However, Rial is no fool. He has a reputation for trickery. I feel he has a surprise for us." Sinbad frowned and added, "I don't like surprises."

Omar's bearded face wrinkled in a smile. "Unless they are your own surprises," he said.

"Nice to have a first mate who understands me," Sinbad said, amused. "Come on; let's see what surprises we can come up with."

On deck, Sinbad motioned to Henri Delacrois, who was wearing his usual fighting leathers. "Be certain that archery team of yours is well supplied with arrows," he said. Next he located the giant Viking. "Ralf, I've been observing you practicing with a sling. It seems large enough to throw a stone as big as my fist. How accurate are you?"

Pleased at the prospect of action, the blond giant shrugged and said, "I can hit a man at one hundred feet, nine times out of ten."

"Very good!" Sinbad congratulated him. "Get six or eight stones from our ballast, and be ready to use them. Wait," he added, "Also get a good pile of pebbles so we'll be ready for anything."

"Aye, sir!" Ralf Gunarson said eagerly and departed his blond beard over his shoulder.

Glancing at Tishimi, whose long black hair was rippling with the breeze, Sinbad said to Omar, "I never have to ask her to be ready."

"Now what?" Omar asked.

In response, Sinbad bellowed, "Helm! Aim for that ship on the horizon!"

"Aye aye, sir!" They were on their way. The ship seemed to respond eagerly as it sliced through the waves.

When the black pirate ship was in full view, the lookout cried, "She's bearing a-port!"

"What in Allah's name?" Omar asked.

"Hold your course!" Sinbad commanded.

"I thought we were going to fight!" Ralf said in dismay.

"He wants us to follow him," Sinbad said flatly. "That's good enough reason to continue on!" He licked his salty lips. "Hold your patience, Ralf and everyone else as well! This isn't over yet, not by a long way."

When the Blue Nymph gained the location where the pirate had veered away, a voice came from the departing black ship. "Running away, Sinbad?" the voice said, amplified by a speaking-trumpet.

They could see the stern of the departing ship, with its wake of green lined with white foam. A dinghy was hanging across the stern. Sinbad inflated his broad chest and replied, "Seems you are the one running away, Rial. When we got close to you, you veered aside."

"I had my reasons, Sinbad! You'll see."

The black ship began to come about.

"Now we can fight!" Ralf said eagerly. "Let us meet them!"

"Maintain course!" Sinbad ordered.

"Why the preparation if we aren't fighting?" Henri Delacrois asked, his trim brown moustache vibrating with anger.

"So we'll be ready when fighting becomes necessary," Sinbad said with flat certainty.

Even as he spoke, the wind died. "Oars!" Sinbad ordered. He saw the oars on the pirate ship come out as well. He also saw the rudder on the black boat swerve. The bow of the opponent began to turn in response. A golden noonday sun burned down on the smooth sea.

To those aching for a fight, it seemed forever before the sleek black form of the pirate's vessel was behind them, broadside to the Blue Nymph. Without warning, three enormous arrows flew toward them. One pierced the limp sail; one hit the Blue Nymph's stern, while the other flew by harmlessly.

Sinbad's keen brown eyes determined these arrows were over three feet long, tipped with flint the size of his hand. "What in Hades was that?" Omar asked.

"A mistake on Rial's part," Sinbad said. Then: "Haroun! What do you see to account for that attack?"

"Large bows attached to the enemy ship's railing," the lookout reported.

"It would take several men to draw such a bow," Sinbad said. "Such a waste."

"How was using it a mistake?" Omar asked.

"We are going directly away from Rial," Sinbad said. "We would make a better target if we were broadside of him. Now that we know he has these weapons, we will try not to give him our broadside." To the lookout he added, "Anything else that looks strange to you?"

"There is something large and covered with canvas on his deck, possibly a huge box."

"Why aren't they shooting more arrows?" Omar asked.

"Rial has seen what I detected, that we offer too slim a target. He would have a limited amount of large arrows available."

"One hit our sail."

"I think Rial knows our sails are double-woven and won't rip from a single tear." Sinbad stared at his opponent's vessel as if trying to see what was under that square of canvas. "I am more concerned about what is hidden."

"We will find out sooner than I like," Omar said. "He has more oarsmen, and his ship is lighter than ours." Even as Omar made that observation, the bow of the pirate ship began to swing toward them.

"Omar, did you notice the dinghy?" Sinbad asked.

"I did. I don't recall the Black Pirate using a dinghy before."

"Nor do I," Sinbad replied, an intent musing look on his face. "I would like to know its purpose."

Less than one hour later, the black pirate ship was within one hundred feet. "Ralf," Sinbad said, "can your sling make that distance?"

The blond young giant grinned. "One way to find out," he said. "What target?"

"That canvas-covered item on the deck," Sinbad said.

Ralf loaded a large stone into his sling and began to spin. Just as he released the sling, crewmen on the other ship yanked the canvas away revealing a cage. Before his missile hit its target, three harpies flew out and were airborne as the rock crashed into the cage.

"These are for you, Sinbad!" Rial shouted gleefully, as the harpies screeched shrilly and flew for the Blue Nymph. "They want your blood!"

"Harpies!" Tishimi cried. "The essence of evil! My blade thirsts for their bodies!"

"Henri!" Sinbad ordered. That was all the archer needed. He and his three team-mates lifted their bows and took aim. The arrows flew true, but the harpies were fast and dodged them.

"Ralf!" Sinbad snapped. In a second the Viking's sling snapped, and a stone passed near one of the flying monsters. "A handful of pebbles!" Sinbad ordered. "Henri! Scatter your arrows!"

The shrieking harpies aimed for Sinbad, but the pebbles and the arrows reached them first. A pebble hit the body of one harpy, who yelped with indignation, but was unharmed. It did, however, dodge away from its goal. An arrow shot through a harpy's wing, but she shrugged it off; still, she changed course. Tishimi swung her sword at the third harpy and cut off a leg. The harpy screamed and fell to the waiting water and the kraken appeared again and caught it, then dived back into the depths.

Unbelieving, the two remaining harpies fluttered in doubt giving Ralf a chance to slam a large rock into one and send it to join its sister. The remaining harpy screamed in misery and flew back to Rial's vessel where the pirate ordered his crew to net it. On his own ship, Sinbad roared with laughter. He sensed that Grachene regretted the missed chance to draw blood.

"Aren't harpies immortal?" Henri asked the attractive Tishimi. She is wearing her usual black silks and leggings.

Tishimi nodded. With a smile, she continued, "As is the kraken. I wonder how the kraken's stomach will deal with this?"

"Helm, bring us about!" Sinbad ordered.

"We fight!" Ralf gloried, flexing his muscles. His leather vest rippled. He checked his broadsword and huge battle axe.

Sinbad noted that Rial was bringing his ship about as well. "Henri, keep arrows flying at their bow rail! Ralf, do the same with your sling! When both of us are broadside, Rial is certain to try his arrow machines again!"

Arrows and stones pelted the pirate's rail containing the threatening bows as the Blue Nymph became broadside of the pirate vessel, then completed the turn and bore straight for Rial.

As the black ship came within range, Omar threw a lighted lamp. It landed on the other ship's deck, broke, and flames erupted. Quickly a pirate grabbed a bit of canvas and slapped it out, and then the mermaid figurehead broached the rail of the pirate ship. Many of Sinbad's crew were in the bow and rushed over to confront Rial's sailors.

Three of Rial's people were busy holding the net that had captured the harpy. The others had swords and scimitars, but Ralf plowed into one cluster of them. He slammed them to the deck, then picked one up by the heels and swung him as if he was the battle axe Ralf had on his belt. Any unfortunate enough to fall over the side found the kraken waiting.

In the close quarter fighting, Henri demonstrated that he was a quality swordsman as well as archer, while Tishimi's magic sword took its toll as she slashed and dodged.

Sinbad spied Rial trying to run to his cabin. He felt Grachene warm with anticipation. Grabbing a dangling sail rope, Sinbad swung up and over the pirate and dropped in front of the door to the cabin. Grinning, Sinbad said, "Trying to get away from us, Rial?"

Grabbing a handful of the pirate's shirt, Sinbad brought Rial's face next to his own. "Who is helping you, Rial?" he snarled.

"Damn you, Sinbad," Rial hissed. "The gods love you!"

"I make my own luck, Rial!" Sinbad snapped back. "You, on the other hand, must have a god helping you else you would not have the harpies." His nose pressed against that of Rial. "You cannot deny it! Who is it, Rial?"

The pirate's face sagged. "There is no way I can tell you, Sinbad. Hit me, stab me, do what you will. Your punishment will be as naught compare to that of a god."

Sinbad knew the pirate was right. While he would enjoy thrashing Rial, there were other questions he wanted answered. He realized he would be wasting time asking Rial. Glancing around, he spotted three red-vested crewmen nearby. "Take this rat and bind and gag him," Sinbad ordered. "Lock him in the cabin."

All of the pirate's crew was subdued, he saw. Motioning Omar over he instructed him, "Have the sail cut down and tossed into the drink," he said. "Ditch all but two of the oars."

"Why not just put the torch to it?" asked Tah, one of Sinbad's older crewmen. He was grim.

Sinbad shook his head. "I have no trouble killing when fighting," he said. "But I don't slaughter the helpless. Leaving them two oars gives them something of a chance."

"How can they use the oars?" Tah asked, motioning at the bound crewmen. "They are all tied up tightly."

Sinbad smiled. "I have no doubt that they will all be free within an hour," he said, and then he eyed Tah. "How long do you think it would take you, in their place?"

Tah cocked his head, and then nodded. "I see your point. Very well; we leave two oars."

"Also," Sinbad added, "move the dinghy to the Blue Nymph."

"How will we hang it?" Tah asked, and then smiled and held up a hand. "Never mind; we'll do it the same way these scoundrels have done."

Sinbad chuckled. "Very good, Tah." Then he changed his attention to the three pirates who were still fighting to keep the harpy within the net.

Tapping one on the shoulder, Sinbad said, "Where did you come from before you saw us?" he asked.

The pirate shook his head. "I can't tell you that," he said.

Sinbad motioned to two nearby crewmen of his. "Take this man and shove him into the net," he ordered. "The harpy needs company."

"You couldn't!" said the startled pirate. "You wouldn'..." At that point, the two crewmen had him by the shoulders. "No!" he screamed. "No! It was the Island of Collapsing Pillars," he said. "We came from there!"

Tishimi was nearby and heard his revelation. She nodded. "I have heard the tale of that evil island," she said. "It is a vicious place."

"How far away would it be?" Sinbad asked the pirate.

"We left at daybreak," the man told him.

Looking around, Sinbad spotted the Viking. "Ralf!" he called. Golden yellow beard over his shoulder, the giant turned to Sinbad. "Can you get this net firmly around the harpy?" Sinbad asked.

With a broad grin, Ralf replied, "My arms are up to it," and came over. In a matter of seconds, he had taken the net from the three pirates and gathered up the net ends. "Done!" he said triumphantly.

To the pirates, Sinbad indicated the broken side of the cage where Ralf's stone had struck. "Repair that," he directed. With a sparkle in his eye he added, "If you don't make a good job of it, the harpy will be glad to escape and repay you for holding the net."

When Sinbad's ship sailed away, several crewmen were busy fixing a place on the stern from which to hang the dinghy, others doing miscellaneous necessary duties, and none but Henri paying any attention to the dwindling pirate ship. "I can't believe they were pirates!" he declared to Tishimi. "Schoolyard children could have put up a better defense."

Standing by Sinbad, Omar grinned at Henri's comment "Sinbad, my fire ball worked just fine."

Smiling, Sinbad said, "Yes, I see the smoke rising from the burning ship as we sail away."

Unperturbed by Sinbad's sarcasm, Omar said, "I only threw one fire ball, just to test it. Next time we will know what to do and burn our opponent down to the water!" He turned away. "Now I have to catch a fish for Samson's meal."

"Smart cat," Sinbad said. "Has you feeding him."

"Not until he caught and ate all the rats on board," Omar said. "We had a deal, and I'm sticking to it. He is a smart cat, by the way."

"Cats have proven their intelligence long ago," Tishimi volunteered softly. "In one country, they have been worshipped. Having people worship them proves their intelligence."

Sinbad laughed. "I can't argue with that. All right, Omar; catch some food for your intelligent partner." Then he turned his attention to Tishimi. "Let's go to my cabin and you can tell me about the collapsing pillars island." Sinbad could sense Grachene's disappointment.

It was cooler in the darkened cabin. They settled into two chairs, Sinbad behind his ornate wooden desk. Tishimi looked at Sinbad's brown face and said, "All my life I have accumulated stories of magical places," she began, took a breath and continued. "I know of few more evil than the Island of the Collapsing Pillars. It is an island with a deep bay. The bay reaches the sea by way of two slanting columns that are shaped like a gigantic V. In the daylight, that is. At night, they close. At night and sometimes in the day."

"Sometimes?"

"When a ship enters the bay, the pillars close immediately."

"Why?"

"So the Cyclops can feed."

"A Cyclops comes out and eats the crew?"

Tishimi shook her head. "Not at first. This Cyclops cannot stand the light. With the pillars closed, the ship will be there at night. The Cyclops is a giant, and sleeps in a big cavern at the end of the bay. It comes out well after sundown. That is when the Cyclops eats." She shuddered.

"If the Cyclops sleeps in the day, couldn't sailors kill him first?"

"There are satyrs on the island with the Cyclops. They raise sheep and cattle for it to eat when he can't get his.." She shuddered again. "...favorite food. If anyone enters his cave, they shriek, throw rocks at the intruders, and keep on until the Cyclops wakens. The cavern is dark, so he can see and capture and eat any foolish enough to come in."

Sinbad lifted a questioning eyebrow. "I thought satyrs were gentle creatures."

"Most are," Tishimi agreed. "These, however, are under the control of Ares and are quite vicious."

"Ares?" Sinbad asked. "Are you certain?"

With a nod, Tishimi said, "There is no doubt of his involvement."

"Then we are in for trouble," Sinbad muttered, rubbing a hand musingly over his Van Dyke beard. He got to his feet, brown eyes looking thoughtful. "Thanks, Tishimi. We'll get there sometime tonight. It would be a good idea for us all to get some rest."

"There is one other thing you should know," Tishimi told him. "Two of the satyrs play the pipes."

"Ah!" Sinbad remarked. "That is more like the satyrs I have heard of."

Tishimi shook her head. Her long black hair rippled. "It is not a good thing, Sinbad; they play the pipes to put you to sleep, so they can take you to the Cyclops, for him to feed."

Sinbad frowned. "That is not good." He thought for a breath, and then added, "We should find wax for the ears. If there is not enough wax, cloth patches to cover ears and keep out the luring sound of the pipes."

"So the Cyclops can feed."

"That would be a worthwhile precaution."

Later, Tishimi was seated on the deck near a rail when Omar came up. He noted that she seemed to be observing something with curiosity. "What has your attention, girl?" Omar asked.

She put a finger to her lips and whispered, "Samson has sensed something," she whispered. "Turn quietly and look toward the captain's cabin."

Omar saw the cat perhaps ten yards away, sitting on the deck in front of the cabin. The door was open, and a large black bird was perched on it. "A raven!" Omar said in amazement.

Tishimi nodded. "I sense some magic about that bird," she said quietly. "You will note that, even though he occasionally washes a paw, Samson is keeping the raven in sight at all times. I feel that Samson knows there is something evil about that black thing."

Even as she spoke, the raven suddenly dove into the cabin. Samson immediately crouched and, as the bird flew out, green cloth pouch in his beak, Samson sprang and caught him in midair. Feathers flew, but the raven didn't live long enough to squawk. The cat stood over the bird a moment, touched it with his nose…and then clamped its head in his jaws and drug it to the side and dropped it overboard.

Tishimi smiled. "I said Samson was an intelligent beast," she said. "He knows that raven is evil and doesn't want to eat it."

She found she was saying that to Omar's back. The First Mate was hurrying to retrieve the purse. Picking it up, he went in search of Sinbad and related what had happened.

Sinbad thought, then gave a solemn nod. "Ares was controlling the raven," he said.

"But why?" asked the First Mate. "Gods have no need of gold."

"It was not riches Ares wanted," Sinbad said, lips tightened. "He is after identification of the goddess helping us," he explained. "The purse would have the undeniable sign of the goddess. Then he could tell the other gods that she had failed in her duties."

"Her duties?"

With a nod, Sinbad explained what Persephone had told him. "Our goal is to recover that golden mask and return it. Ares doesn't want that to happen. Again," he added, "we must get rest before we reach that cursed island."

Their rest was disturbed as the blazing sun neared the horizon. Suddenly black clouds appeared, lightning dancing below their darkness.

Omar shouted, "Lower the sail! Tie everything down! We're in for a rough one!"

In the commotion, he saw Samson bowed up, hissing at the clouds. Then the cat scurried to the hold. Omar looked at Sinbad, who was standing beside him. "This isn't just any storm," he muttered. "Samson seemed to sense evil."

Nodding, Sinbad said, "An evil known as Ares," he said, and explained what Tishimi had told him. "He would like to sink us before we reach the Island of the Collapsing Pillars."

Clenching his teeth, Omar said, "Why bother? From what you say, that island will get us in any case."

A hard smile tightened Sinbad's face. "Old friend, I think this storm is a compliment. It means Ares fears we can subdue the Cyclops and the satyrs." As he spoke, a bolt of lightning struck the sea ahead of them and an explosion of thunder shook the Blue Nymph.

"Bring down the mast!" Omar shouted when the rumble died away. "It could attract lightning! Bring it down and secure it to the deck!"

"Tie yourselves to lengths of rope!" Sinbad added. "Those washed overboard can then be recovered!" Omar nodded his approval.

The storm was like a gigantic black dragon, the lightning being the flames it spat and the thunder was its roar. Wind and sea crashed over the Blue Nymph as sailors tied the mast into place. Omar had tied a rope around his own waist and offered one to Sinbad. Sinbad waved it away. "I'll manage," he growled, hands clamped on a railing. The wind whipped stinging pellets of water against his face as his ship rolled in the waves. Lightning flared, illuminating the tossing deck, empty save for the helmsman who had lashed himself to the helm. Thunder boomed.

"Do your worst, Ares!" Sinbad shouted. "I'm going on!"

In response, there was another burst of lightning, this one so close Sinbad was momentarily blinded. He blinked, and then shook his fist at the sky.

"You would defy a god, Sinbad?" Persephone asked in his mind.

Sinbad's first impulse was to answer a sharp "Yes!" but then he paused, remembering the time Omar grabbed his head and shook it and said a god was affecting him. After a brief contemplation, he said. "I might defy a god, but that would be senseless, wouldn't it?"

There was amusement in Persephone's answer. "There are times when insanity, with assistance, can achieve much."

Smiling into the wind, Sinbad replied, "I'll welcome any assistance available."

Then Persephone was gone.

Saying nothing to Omar, Sinbad took the rope from him and lashed it around his waist.

Was the lightning a bit weaker? Did the rain and wind slacken? Wasn't the Blue Nymph moving more smoothly through the sea? Sinbad wondered if Persephone had somehow coerced Zephyr's assistance.

The final blast of lightning revealed an island ahead of them.

"Helm! Circle the island and look for a beach," Sinbad ordered. Seeing Omar's questioning look, he said, "The water will be too deep to anchor at the pillars. If there is a beach, the water will be shallower there, so that we can anchor."

"Of course," Omar agreed.

There was a chill as they neared the island, a chill that was not from the wind on their wet clothing. Omar shook his head somberly and said. "This is indeed a place of evil."

"Evil that is determined to see we fail in our goal," Sinbad agreed through tightened lips. With determination he finished, "But we shall succeed!"

"That we will," Omar agreed starkly. Then he straightened. "I need to check for damage. I'll report when I complete the check."

When the First Mate returned, there was a look on his face that alerted Sinbad. "What is it, Omar? What is wrong?"

"There was very little trouble, Sinbad, but one loss that is important: A water barrel lost its bung and leaked out. Perhaps we can make our return trip without it, but its loss concerns me."

They were interrupted by a call from the sailor in the crow's nest. "Beach ahead!" he shouted.

Storm clouds had moved away and a glimpse of moonlight reflected on white sand at the edge of the island. "Move in closer and drop anchors," Omar ordered. The Blue Nymph neared the beach, and then there was a double splash as two anchors plunged into the waters. The giant weights went down; hit, dragged, and then the ship shuddered slightly as the anchors caught.

"There is yet time for some rest," Sinbad proclaimed. Entering his cabin he got into his hammock. There was no sound of pipes from shore, but he didn't need them. Closing his eyes, he was immediately asleep.

Sinbad found himself, Omar, Tishimi, Henri and Ralf at the opening of a great dry valley. It was because of the dryness that each of them had a goatskin waterbag on their backs. He led them into the valley and, as they were within it, an abrupt landslide sealed the entrance behind them.

"That is not good," Omar said.

"We are all alive," Sinbad replied. "We continue on."

They were all sweating as they followed the stone path between the steep valley walls. Then, unexpectedly, a flying snake dove at Sinbad. His sword flashed and, to his surprise, the snake divided into two separate snakes! He swung again, and there were four. Recognizing it as magic, Sinbad called: "Tishimi!"

Tishimi was beside him then, her magic blade swinging. All the snakes died.

"You must live, Sinbad. This is a magical vision, but die here and you really die!" she murmured.

Sinbad understood her warning; even to understanding this was all a dream. It did not change his intent to move forward to their goal.

They followed a path that led around a bend in the valley, and a huge Minotaur appeared to block their way. Sinbad swung his sword, dodging to the side as he swung. Even with his speed, he barely moved in time to avoid the Minotaur's massive horns.

Henri rapidly launched a series of arrows at the beast, but the Minotaur was able to deflect them with his horns. Ralf slammed his battle ax against the monster but, again, it met the blows with its horns. Then Tishimi managed to contact with her magic sword and, suddenly, the Minotaur vanished.

At the end of the valley they found a table made by a slab of rock that sat atop two stones. On it was a bronze lamp. Feeling caution was needed, Sinbad approached the table slowly, stopping at the edge. Nothing happened, so he reached out a hand, touched the lamp.

And a gigantic cloud of dust erupted with a boom and grew, and grew, and became a huge and monstrous genie, so large that his arm was thicker than a water barrel and the top of his round head reached twice the height of the Blue Nymph's crow's nest. "Who disturbs me?" he roared in evident anger, and the sound of his voice echoed down the valley. Sinbad noted that a random breeze rippled the genie's body and that some dust blew away. He also realized that, within his wavering body, the genie was gradually intensifying.

Sinbad remembered a trick he had played as a child. "Water!" he shouted, pulling the goatskin waterbag off of his shoulder. He aimed the spout at the giant and squeezed the bag, his thumb angled on the spout. A silvery spear of water pierced the genie's legs, and then Sinbad changed the way his thumb angled and gave a harder squeeze. A fan of water washed away more dust and mud ran like blood down the twisting inner growth of the monster.

With his mighty strength, Ralf sprayed water into the genie's stomach, as the giant screamed. Tishimi squirted water as she strode rapidly up to the writhing genie and she then dropped the waterbag and slashed her magic sword into the part that was forming.

Splashed by more water from Omar and Henri, the giant dissolved.

There was still a small amount of water in Sinbad's bag. He used it to wash the lamp until it was shining. He held it up and grinned at his followers. "We have succeeded!" he exclaimed.

Then the lamp disappeared in a flash of light, a flash that intensified until Sinbad realized it was the light of morning.

When Sinbad rolled out of the hammock, he was pleased but felt that he was as tired as when he had first crawled in. He washed his face in cold water, then went on deck. He was standing at the beachside railing when Omar joined him.

"There is a stream of fresh water," the First Mate said jubilantly, pointing at the beach.

Sinbad had been studying the stream himself. It flowed down a steep slope that led to the beach. Up the slope there was a stone ledge. A sheet of water overflowed the stone. Bushes grew around the rear of the ledge. Beyond the bushes a few feet, the slope resumed its ascent.

A satyr came out on the ledge and grinned toward Sinbad and Omar. The satyr tossed a rock into the unseen pool on the ledge, and water splashed upward. The satyr pointed at the pool, grinned again, then slid into the bushes beyond the ledge.

"I get the message," Sinbad said to Omar in sarcasm tinged with humor. "The satyr's wanting us to come and get the water. It wanted to be sure we know the pool is at the ledge." Sinbad sighed. "It was already obvious the water was there, but the satyr wanted to make certain." He looked levelly at Omar. "I estimate that the dinghy can carry a water barrel and no more than three others or it would be overloaded when the barrel is full. I'm considering taking you and Tishimi with me. What do you think?"

Omar considered Sinbad's proposition for a moment and then said, "I would think any of us could take on at least three satyrs. If Henri and his arrow crew cover us, as well as the Viking and his sling, we could even take on the Cyclops."

Tightening his lips, Sinbad murmured, "Remember; the satyrs and the Cyclops are under the control of Ares. We have no real idea of what they might do. Besides," he added, focusing on the slope, "there is other ammunition they can use against us."

Omar looked at the landscape. Above the pool, there were rocks and even boulders thrusting out. The First Mate nodded. "A potential landslide," he said. "If we were at the pool, filling our barrel, we would have no defense." He rubbed his bearded chin. "Let me think on it. Meanwhile, I'll have Tah and a couple of others lower the dinghy and bring it around."

Soon the dinghy was rowed to a place beneath the rail where Sinbad stood. Omar was standing in the small boat. He looked up at Sinbad. "Any ideas?" he asked.

Sinbad nodded, as Omar climbed a rope ladder to his side. "Under the ledge," Sinbad said. "It is large enough to shelter three people from the falling stones."

Omar studied the scene, and then nodded. "I can fashion a rope harness for the barrel, so it can be held beneath the ledge." He smiled with appreciation at Sinbad. "It will work!"

"Find Tishimi," Sinbad said. "Find wax, as well."

Grey eyebrows lifted, Omar asked, "Wax?"

Sinbad explained about the pipes that could cast the spell of sleep. "Also," he added, "have Tah bring the signal drum to the deck and start a continuous drumming when the satyrs appear. That, I hope, will keep the spell of the pipes from affecting our crew."

"It might be that the magic of sleep won't carry across the water," Omar said.

"That is a possibility," Sinbad agreed. "However, I prefer caution over chance. Find Tishimi and the wax."

Sinbad looked around and spotted Henri. Approaching him, he asked, "Any chance arrows could reach that ledge above the beach?"

Henri eyed the location, then held a wet finger up to test the air. "So long as the wind is still or, better, blowing toward the beach."

"Very good. There is a good chance we shall need you." Then Sinbad searched out Ralf and told him to be at the rails as well, with rocks and pebbles available.

When Sinbad returned to the rope ladder leading to the dinghy, Tishimi was there as was Omar, who had brought beeswax with him. As the three got into the dinghy, a wind abruptly began, blowing straight from the beach.

"That will affect our arrows," Henri called. "But it may drop."

Jaw tightened, Sinbad said, "I doubt it will slacken," he said to Omar. "I feel Ares is behind its appearance."

"I think you are correct," Omar muttered glumly. They rowed to the beach.

Sinbad and Omar manned the oars, while Tishimi held the water barrel in place.

When they beached the small boat, Sinbad stood looking at the roll of rope at the bow, rope to tie the dinghy in place. Detaching the rope from the bow, Sinbad said, "Change in plans. This rope looks long enough to reach above the ledge." He bent over and tied the rope to the harness Omar had placed around the wooden container. "We can leave the barrel here, to the side, where it will be safe from any landslide."

"Good idea," Omar said.

"I sense the satyrs!" Tishimi exclaimed. "Best to plug our ears now."

"Agreed!" Sinbad said, taking a small amount of the wax. "Protect your ears, and we climb up to the ledge."

Tishimi held up a slender hand. "They're near," she cautioned. "I sense magic."

Omar shrugged, put wax plugs in his ears, and began the ascent. Sinbad, holding the rope tied to the barrel, let Tishimi start upward, and then followed. They were halfway to the top when a vibration reached Sinbad. Despite his ear-plugs, he found himself succumbing to the evil magic. At the same time, he noted that Tishimi, sword in hand, was not affected. Reaching out his left hand, he touched her magic blade.

The threatening numbness disappeared.

Noting his actions, Tishimi slowly extended her sword to touch the side of Omar, who was also showing signs of giving in to sleep.

Starting with a flinch, Omar looked back at the Oriental woman and smiled his thanks.

As they mounted the ledge, they were engulfed by satyrs.

Omar's broad arms swept some aside, while Tishimi's enchanted blade took the lives of several and so did the sword of Sinbad. They regained their feet, still surrounded, still fighting. Then a large stone from Ralf's sling tore into one satyr, sending him backward into another.

Flashing a look on thanks over his shoulder, Sinbad fought on, while satyrs began to beat a hasty retreat.

Sinbad took the wax from his ears and motioned for the others to do the same. Quickly he pulled the barrel up the slope and it was quickly filled.

Then the ground began to rumble. Fastening the barrel's bung, Sinbad said, "Under the ledge!" Before he joined them, the tied the rope to an outcropping of stone, making certain the rope length was sufficient, he started the barrel's roll downhill then ducked under the ledge as rocks and then boulders began to roll toward them.

The ledge was barely enough shelter. Glancing down, Sinbad saw that the barrel was bouncing to the side, as he had hoped. The landslide would not harm it.

Aside from a few pebbles and sand, nothing struck the three huddled below the shelf of rock.

When nothing else fell, Sinbad led Omar and Tishimi down the slope. Once a loud roar came from above. "The Cyclops has been awakened," Sinbad said. "He expresses his displeasure. As the sun still shines, he offers no threat."

Returning to the dinghy, they rowed back to the Blue Nymph. Sinbad and Omar lifted the water barrel to the waiting Ralf, who took it with a smile. "I got a couple of those creatures," he bragged.

"If the wind had lessened, my arrows would have found many!" Henri said in bitter disappointment.

When Omar and Sinbad met in the captain's cabin, Omar asked, "What plans have occurred to you, Sinbad? How should we approach this?"

Stroking his beard thoughtfully, Sinbad mused, "I think I know why they carried a dinghy. With Ares in control, they could enter the bay safely. The dinghy would be easiest. They rowed it in, found a hiding place, put the mask away, and returned to the ship."

"You think we could do the same?"

"Emphatically not!" Sinbad exclaimed, shaking his head. "We would have no way to defend ourselves, no back-up support, if we used the dinghy." He took a deep breath and then sighed. "We have no choice but to sail into the trap and see what we can do."

"It is still daylight. I understood the pillars stayed open until dark."

"Or until a ship enters the bay," Sinbad said.

Omar's eyes widened. "Oh!" He ran his fingers through his grey beard, then added, "So what do we do now?"

"For one thing, the sooner we start the better. The Cyclops won't come out in daylight, which will give us an hour or so to search for the mask."

"We find the mask, then fight the Cyclops when he wades out to our ship, right?"

Sinbad nodded. "For one thing, Henri and Ralf can use their weapons against him."

"If I recall correctly, the Cyclops all have a rather thick skin."

"That's why they'll be ordered to aim for his eye!" Sinbad opened the cabin door and looked back at Omar. "Get us going as quickly as possible. We need all the daylight we can get."

Sinbad looked for Tah and found him at the far end of the deck. "Did you hear the music of the pipes," he asked, "or did your drum drown the sounds out?"

Tah's expression darkened. "Oh, I heard them all right," he said. "The sound was shrill and pierced the rhythm of the drum like an arrow through smoke."

"Did they make you sleepy?"

Satisfaction brightened Tah's face. "No, they did not. None of the crew drowsed off."

Sinbad nodded his own satisfaction. "Then the magic does not reach as far as the sound," he said. "That is good to know."

The indigo sail of the Blue Nymph was raised, and the mighty ship sailed away from the beach. As they sailed, Sinbad went to Henri. "When we near the collapsing pillars, have your archers ever alert for satyrs," he ordered. "Especially satyrs carrying pipes."

Henri nodded.

Next Sinbad located Ralf and gave him the same orders. Grinning above his golden yellow beard, the Viking said, "I'll have some large rocks with their name on them!"

Sinbad shook his head. "Just pebbles, Ralf. We need to save the larger stones for Cyclops."

The Viking took a breath, then relaxed and said, "I understand."

As the Blue Nymph cut a wake through the choppy sea, Sinbad went to Tishimi. She was seated quietly on the deck, squinting in thought as she poised a pen over a small sheet of parchment. "Another poem?"

Tishimi lifted her emerald gaze to Sinbad. "Yes," she murmured, "but I'm having a problem. So far, I have –

> Satyrs danced on the island,
> Doing an evil thing

"But I can't complete it."

Sinbad cocked his head in thought, then said,

> "Then with the help of a magic blade,
> Were conquered by the Oriental maid."

Tishimi smiled. "I thank you, kind sir, but my poems aren't to glorify me." Then, in a more serious mode, she added, "But I don't believe you

...the mighty ship sailed away from the beach.

came to help me with my poetry. How can I be of help, Captain Sinbad?"

"You have a way of sensing magic, Tishimi." He pointed ahead, where waves were washing against the base of the pillars, not far ahead. "We are going between those pillars in search of a magic object I believe is hidden inside. Is there a chance your knowledge of magic can help us locate that?"

Tishimi contemplated the question, then replied, "It is possible. However, this entire island vibrates with evil magic. That could complicate matters."

"Understood," Sinbad said. "However, the object we are looking for is not evil, but the magic of the gods. Will that help?"

Tishimi watched as the Blue Nymph soared forward, passing the side of a pillar. "Possibly," she admitted. "Possibly."

When the ship curved to face the open pillars, Sinbad noted the lowering sun and estimated there were two hours of light remaining. He was pleased to see that Henri and his crew of archers, as well as Ralf with his sling, were standing at readiness; a readiness immediately called for as two satyrs showed up on one of the pillars.

There was a ledge there, and an opening in the pillar. Two satyrs danced out, each holding a pipe. As they appeared, they were met by a barrage of arrows and stones. One satyr fell into the sea, and the other collapsed lifeless on the ledge.

A great roar of approval arose from Sinbad's crew.

The feeling of triumph disappeared when the Blue Nymph entered the waters of the dark blue bay and the pillars slammed together behind them. The waters shook with the violence of the sudden closure.

High rocky cliffs surrounded the bay. The lowered sun didn't reach over the top, so the bay was in full shade as the Blue Nymph sailed in. There were slits and cracks in the rock, scattered ledges, the dark opening of several caves. Two of the caves had a ledge beneath them, and the arrangement suggested a grinning death's head, causing shudders from some of the crew.

Sinbad was not unfamiliar with magic, and could sense the evil Tishimi had mentioned.

"Remain alert!" Sinbad ordered, then added, "Tah, lower the dinghy and bring it to the side. Ralf, I want you and Tishimi with me." He went to where the rope ladder hung, and the two met him there. Thinking the cracks and slits could be a good place to hide the mask; Sinbad obtained a gaff hook with a long staff and carried it as he went down the ladder.

When all three were on the dinghy, Sinbad said, "Ralf, I need your mighty strength to man the oars on this small boat. Sit on the middle bench, put the paddles in their oarlocks, and take us to the nearest cliff." He looked at Tishimi. "As I have informed you, I need your instincts to help locate the hidden mask."

Tishimi nodded. "I will do my best."

Cautioned by the fate of their kin, satyrs either remained hidden or peeked quickly out of various cave mouths, chittering shrill curses on Sinbad and his crew.

"It would be quite difficult to ascend these steep slopes," Sinbad said, "so I feel the mask will be in a place easily reached."

Tishimi agreed. "There were no magicians on the black pirate ship, so levitation could not have been used."

As the sky overhead began to darken, Ralf rowed them along beside the base of the stone wall. Sinbad extended the gaff hook into crevices. For an hour, their efforts were fruitless, other than disturbing some bats and some snakes. Then Sinbad's probe touched something else, something that did not react by slithering or flying away. Carefully, Sinbad pulled out the gaff, and a black silk bag was hanging from it.

"Success!" Ralf shouted.

Taking the bag off the hook, Sinbad felt it. "I don't think so," he muttered. "This doesn't seem heavy enough to be gold." Opening the bag, he pulled out a tin mask of a satyr.

"Someone is pulling a trick on us," he said. Then he dropped the gaff and pulled out his sword as a batch of snakes shot out of the same place. "Deadly poisonous snakes!" Sinbad warned, slashing at them with his sword. "Don't let them even nick you!"

Despite the smallness of their boat, Tishimi and Ralf joined the battle, magic sword and battle axe swinging in unison with Sinbad's blade. One snake made it aboard, but Sinbad's boot smashed its head. Chips of rock flew as the booming assault of Ralf's battle axe destroyed more of the vicious and hissing creatures. Shrill satyr cackling issued from the caves and echoed around the enclosed bay.

Then two more snakes appeared. These spread membranous wings and flew!

The flying serpents were swift, and dodged both swords and battle axe as they darted about. When they neared, they would emit a squirt of deadly venom which the trio avoided. On the spur of the moment, Sinbad untwirled his turban, then jumped into the air at the slithery venomous things and caught them in the material of his turban.

As he fell back, Sinbad's marvelous reflexes came into play when he realized he was going to land on the side of their small vessel, which might send his companions into the dark bay. Pulling up his feet, Sinbad plunged into the murky darkness of the waters.

Even the abrupt shock of the icy water did not cause him to release the cloth of his turban and the squirming things within it. Finding their slim bodies with one hand, he squeezed until they moved no more.

With a strong kick of his muscular legs, Sinbad shot to the surface and splashed up beside the dinghy.

At last all the serpents were dead.

Sinbad tossed his turban into the little boat, started to swing one leg over the side, when something from the depths, something feeling like a tentacle, grasped his right ankle. Ralf was about to offer a hand. "A moment," Sinbad gasped, swallowed a deep breath, then dived back down into the nearly freezing water. He pulled a quiveringly eager Grachene from his sash. Bending, he slashed at the tentacle and it parted. He started to return to the surface, but another tentacle imprisoned his left arm. Cursing to himself, Sinbad slashed the other tentacle, and then feeling urged on by the dagger, he turned and plunged toward the source of his distraction.

Something huge loomed in the dark water and Sinbad swung a gleeful Grachene again and again until the creature sank. He wasn't certain he had killed it, but knew it was leaving. In another moment, he returned to the surface, accepted Ralf's offered assistance, and was back aboard the dinghy at last.

Grachene seemed satisfied.

"Was that it? Now we move on?" asked Ralf, going to the oars.

Sinbad inhaled, paused, and looked at Tishimi. "What do you think?" he asked the Oriental girl. "Do you sense anything here?"

Tishimi closed her eyes and took a slow, deep breath. Then her emerald eyes shot open, and she said, "Yes! You were correct, Sinbad; this was a trick but it was a double trick! I feel magic emanating from that same spot."

Sinbad nodded. "That thought had occurred to me," he said softly as he rewrapped his turban and put it on. Taking the gaff, he again explored the narrow cavity. A few rocks fell from above, but ceased when a swarm of arrows swept the caves above.

"That proves we're on the right track," Sinbad said as he pushed the gaff even further than before. He could tell it had contacted something. Pulling the gaff back, they all saw the black bag caught on its hook.

Then Sinbad turned to the giant Viking. "This is the real reason I wanted you along, Ralf. I have been told the mask will lure a human to put it on, and then your spirit is lost. When I retrieve the bag, I must open it to ascertain it is the object we are after. Regardless of what I say, I want you to yank it out of my hand and stuff it into the bag. Understood?"

Grimly, Ralf nodded his blond head. "As you command, Sinbad."

"Why don't I open the mysterious bag?" Tishimi said. "I am quite familiar with magic."

"That is exactly the reason I don't want you to do it," Sinbad explained. "I fear your familiarity with magic could make you susceptible to it. This is not evil magic but some other exercise of godly powers." Taking the black silk bag from the gaff, Sinbad looked at Ralf and added, "Now!"

He opened the silk carefully, feeling the weight of something heavy inside. A glimpse of gold appeared. Slowly Sinbad pulled the cloth down.

"The Golden Mask of Adonis!" he exclaimed and, as he said it, the realization that he must put it on filled his mind. With great willpower, he managed to gasp, "Ralf!"

The Viking giant pulled the silk bag away from Sinbad who, thanks solely to his great control of his mind, he didn't try to retain. Ralf had taken the bag by its edge, and the golden mark fell back inside.

Sinbad slumped to the floor of the dinghy, shaking his head. After taking a deep breath, he looked up. "Thank you, Ralf. You saved my soul." Inhaling again, he said, "Back to the ship! Darkness is coming quickly."

Climbing the rope ladder, Sinbad quickly went to his quarters and slipped the silk bag containing the mask into a drawer with a lock. Only he and Omar had keys to it. Even as he locked the drawer, a mighty roar echoed between the high cliffs surrounding the bay, indicating the arrival of the Cyclops.

On deck, Sinbad saw Tah rushing to the front of the Blue Nymph, the part of the ship facing the approaching monster. Tah drew his sword as he ran. Sinbad was behind him as Tah reached the mermaid figurehead and shouted, "Come taste my sword, you hairless monster!"

The Cyclops was totally hairless; not only bald, but with no body hair. It stood in the water in front of the ship, the bay's surface reaching to its waist. Fully fifty feet rose above the water. As Tah waved his sword, an enormous hand lashed out and swept Tah off the bow.

"No!" Sinbad shouted, crouching, and slamming his feet down to launch himself at the great hand.

Even though the Cyclops had tough skin, Sinbad's body slammed against the back of the giant fist and his fingers dug into the flesh. Tightening the fingers of his left hand, Sinbad used his right to pull an eager Grachene out of his sash.

Tah was wiggling and twisting and shouting as Sinbad swung the dagger down and buried it to the hilt in the ball of Cyclops' thumb.

The monster screamed a piercing cry that filled the cliff-ringed area. Sinbad had hoped the pain would cause the Cyclops to release Tah; he did, but not as Sinbad hoped. He slung his arm out and threw Tah against a stony wall. Tah hit with a life-ending smash.

"You evil beast!" Sinbad yelled, twisting the joyful Grachene deeper into the Cyclops' thumb.

In response, the Cyclops shook his hand violently, shaking Sinbad into the dark waters below.

Sputtering, Sinbad rose to the surface and quickly swam to his ship. As he swam he recalled the dream about the dust genie. "Water was its weakness," he murmured to himself. As he climbed the rope ladder he added, "Light is the Cyclops' weakness."

Gaining the deck, Sinbad shouted, "Omar! Gather all your fireballs!"

In a few seconds, Omar had the lamps on deck and began lighting them because he had realized what Sinbad's purpose was. "Ralf! Henri! Grab some lamps. We're going to light that hideous thing!"

Getting his own lamps, Sinbad ordered, "Now!"

The Cyclops was surprised at the many bursts of flame that sprouted on his vast body; surprised, and hurt. He screamed and writhed in agony. Then he shrunk, and sank lifelessly into the bay. The deck rang with the victorious cries of the crew of the Blue Nymph.

After a joyous celebration, Sinbad went to his quarters.

Persephone was waiting for him.

It didn't surprise Sinbad that she was holding the silk bag that contained the magical mask. "A successful task, Sinbad," she told him. "I am not surprised." From her gown she retrieved the green bag that had financed the trip. Sinbad wondered if Omar had realized its disappearance. "This bag will deliver ten gold pieces for each of your crew, as well as the proper amount for families of the deceased. Then it will produce no more. Each of your deceased crew will go to the Elysian Fields, to await their families."

Lifting the precious black silk bag, she continued, "Now I shall put this where it belongs."

"No," Sinbad contradicted his voice soft but firm. "That alone would not close this matter," he continued to Persephone's startled face. "Listen to my suggestion."

After his explanation, Persephone beamed her approval. "You are a very clever man, Sinbad! It shall be done as you suggest." Persephone disappeared. Sinbad didn't bother to check the locked drawer, as he was certain the silk bag had been returned there.

He located Omar and explained the plan.

The Blue Nymph left when the pillars opened and then assumed the course Sinbad directed. One day later, they saw a fog ahead of them, a fog that trembled with magic. "In … there?" Omar asked hesitantly.

Sinbad nodded. "In there is our destination."

It seemed that even the Blue Nymph quivered as they entered the eerie mist.

When they emerged, an island was ahead of them, an island of tiers of stone that rose at least one hundred feet into the air. There was no beach, only a small opening that curved over the clear water. Sinbad nodded at it. "Lower the dinghy," he said. "I go in there alone. Omar, once I'm inside take the Nymph around to the other side of the island."

"You're going in alone?" the First Mate queried, a look of concern on his face.

"Yes," Sinbad replied. The black silk bag was inside his sash, opposite a calm Grachene. "I'll be met inside."

Understanding dawned on Omar's features. "An unnamed personage, I assume?"

"Exactly."

The dinghy was lowered; Sinbad boarded it and then put the oars into the water. The stone arch was barely high enough for the dinghy to slide under.

Inside, Sinbad paused. Sunlight penetrating the water and painted a wash of shades of blue on the grotto inside. The water was so clear that he could see the bottom. It was as if his small rowboat was floating on air instead of water.

Then Sinbad looked around the grotto. It was high ceilinged and, as he had been told, to the left was a rocky passageway that curved further in. He rowed to it, entered it, and continued on. In a few beats of his paddles he saw more mist. In the mist was a glowing spot of bright gold. Sinbad rowed into it, the glow being his destination.

The voice of Persephone came to his mind. "Hurry," the goddess of the Underworld said. "The expected vessel is entering the outside mist even now."

Soon the glow became an alcove in the stony wall, a small one with a flat ledge. Sinbad went to it, took out the black silk bag and placed it on the ledge.

One single note of welcome sounded as Sinbad placed the mask where it belonged. The golden glow increased. Moving back, Sinbad took his small boat to a darkened area and waited. The glow was now fainter, but visible.

Eventually Sinbad heard the sound of oars dipping into the clear water. Due to the mist, he could see nothing, which was quite as well as it meant that whoever was approaching could not see him. When the glow diminished, he knew it meant the newcomer had removed the mask.

Hearing the retreating sound of paddles stroking the water, Sinbad left his hiding place and followed, sculling his little vessel from the stern to avoid sending sounds of his approach. He cleared the mists just in time to see a small rowboat disappear around the entry curve of the passageway. Sinbad carefully approached that curve, then moved his boat up to the wall and waited.

It only took seconds.

"Very good, Rial!" boomed the voice of Ares. "I knew you were worth saving. Again you have obtained the Mask of Apollo. The embarrassment of Persephone is guaranteed!"

Digging his oars into the water, Sinbad sent his boat shooting out into the grotto. Ares' face was a red blob on the blue walls. "I think not!" Sinbad declared.

Ares' eyes widened, and then he smiled. "Perfect!" he said. "Now I can have the satisfaction of seeing Sinbad defeated! Rial, here is a bow with a magic arrow made to kill Sinbad. Use it!"

Sinbad felt a tingling throb from Grachene and an eagerness. As Rial cocked his bow and sent the magic arrow at Sinbad, he flashed Grachene from its resting place in his sash. On its own, the dagger guided Sinbad's hand. Waving the magic blade back and forth, Sinbad felt intense satisfaction as Grachene sliced the arrow into wasted pieces.

Frowning, Ares said, "You have Grachene! This damned mist prevents me from detecting such. Nonetheless, Sinbad, I shall destroy you myself!"

"I think not!"

Persephone appeared in the air in front of Sinbad.

"Ah, the goddess of the Underworld," Ares said, his voice dripping with sarcasm. "Am I not sending enough souls to you, Persephone?"

"You send many souls, god of War," Persephone said, ice in her voice. "But you will not send Sinbad this day!"

Ares face carried a broad, anticipatory smile. "You think you can best me, Persephone? Shall we proceed with this farce?"

Again, the grotto rang with an emphatic, "I think not!"

The statement was intensified by a bright glow that filled half the area. Zeus, father of the gods, had appeared.

Ares gaped in astonishment and surprise. "F-father," he stammered. "I was but trying to reveal that Persephone is not fulfilling her duties of protecting the mighty mask. That is, you can see how she failed…"

"You are as tricky and devious as Odin's Loki," Zeus thundered. "It is obvious what you have done, Ares. I shall spare Rial," he added, "as he was merely a weak tool you used. Begone!"

Ares vanished and Rial began rowing away, a grateful expression on his humbled face. Sinbad knew he would later face an even more determined Black Pirate, but he felt confident.

"Wait!" Zeus ordered.

Rial froze.

"You have something to return!" Zeus said.

Shamefacedly, Rial held up the bag of black silk.

"I shall take that," Persephone said, drifting to Rial. She lifted the bag from his trembling hand. "I will put it back where it belongs," she said, and floated to the passageway.

"I thank you, Father of Gods," Sinbad murmured.

With a smile, Zeus said, "Sinbad, you do quite well without our help! However, when one of my own strays, I feel obliged to step in."

Persephone returned. "This plan was of Sinbad's creation, Father," she said. "My original intention was merely to return the mask to its proper place. Sinbad suggested this trap to reveal to you the guilt of Ares."

"As we all know, Sinbad is a very worthy man," Zeus said. Then he added, "Now I go."

When Zeus left, Sinbad turned to Persephone. "Should I now return Grachene to you?"

Persephone smiled. "As I said when I passed him to you, Grachene has a mind of his own. At present, he is pleased with you and will leave only when he is ready."

Touching the dagger's handle, Sinbad said, "Grachene is a worthy companion in battle."

"As are you, Sinbad," Persephone said. "I was fortunate to have chosen you for this task." With another smile, she said, "I go now. Your Blue Nymph is even now returning to take you."

"Before you go, I wish to thank you for taking Tah and my other lost crewman to the Elysian Fields."

"It was but what they deserved, Sinbad. Now, farewell!" She faded away.

Satisfied, Sinbad gripped the oars. Another task had ended successfully.

THE END

THE STORY BEHIND
THE STORY

When I saw Ron Fortier's announcement that Airship 27 wanted Sinbad stories, impulse took over.

I've always enjoyed Sinbad. I've seen many Sinbad movies, and the swashbuckling grabbed me; that's probably why I became a fan of Space Opera, because the heroes were often great swashbucklers, even tho they might use ray gun pistols instead of swords and space ships instead of galleons.

Before thinking any further, I requested the Sinbad 'bible' so I would know the setting and characters. There was one problem: Ron wanted fifteen thousand words and for the last year or so my stories had been running around five thousand words. I had my work cut out for me. With the setting and the major characters, it was time to get going.

Well, Sinbad often got involved with the gods, so I decided to have a god/Goddess give him a quest. A Golden Mask with mythical powers sounded good. I decided to use Grecian myth, while not ignoring the others. Of course, I kept Ray Harryhausen in mind for his great monster scenes. Ron had warned me not to introduce a new permanent character, so I created one who became a major character in his own right – and didn't want to kill him off! After a bit of thought, I introduced one who could, on his own, decide to skip – while leaving it where he could be used again, if anyone chose to. He was a fighter created by the gods himself and designed for fighting.

Of course, another god would be fighting against Sinbad and his crew, along with mythical characters such as the hippocamp, the kraken, harpies, amazingly evil satyrs, and climaxing with Cyclops. Plus there had to be a magical and deadly setting. (I even used Morpheus, although I didn't give him credit.) I put in human conflict with the Black Pirate being after revenge on Sinbad.

You say that, with all that, I should have enough for a novel? Hardly; my colorful surroundings were done with an economy of style and a page of action was packed into a single paragraph. All of which is a complete reversal of my lifelong style; years back, my wife said that I would make the Gettysburg Address as long as Gone With the Wind.

No more.

While on a mystical errand, there was a severe limit on help for Sinbad. At one point the Black Pirate says something to the effect: "With your luck, Sinbad, you have the gods behind you!" Sinbad responds, quite truthfully, "I make my own luck!" After succeeding with his quest, while his powerful sponsor is satisfied, Sinbad suggests a more powerful climax and is congratulated on his idea by Zeus. Of course, it works and all live magically ever after...

SHELBY VICK - Was born in 1928 and raised on ballads and Alice In Wonderland, Hiawatha, Flash Gordon, Prince Valiant as well as Saturday matinees at the local movies. There he met Buck Rogers, Zorro, and all those other old-time heroes. Then he found the Oz series as well as pulp magazines, and he was on his way. He has written ever since he discovered pencils and paper. Selling five kid's fantasy shorts and, later, four action paperbacks which, he says, are just as well forgotten. When 'Real life' interfered, he spent many years as a MetLife financial planner, then more as a field man at the county Property Appraiser's Office. A serious auto accident brought about an unplanned retirement. (He was in his seventies, but that hadn't caused him to consider retirement; he was enjoying what he was doing!)

Since January of 2005, he has been publishing Planetary Stories, 'The Return of Space Opera'. As time went by, he added Pulp Spirit and the fantasy magazine, Wonderlust. www.planetarystories.com will get the index page, where you can click on both current and past issues. Spending eight to ten hours each day on his computer, he's happily working more than ever!

MORE VOYAGES!

by Ron Fortier

Every now and then we put together a book that appeals as much to our cadre of writers and artists as it does to our loyal readers. Such a book was "Sinbad –The New Voyages Vol I." Our crew on that first voyage did such a remarkable job with their stories and illustrations that word of the fun they had spread through out our community of talented creators. The stories by Derrick Ferguson, Nancy Hansen and Ian Watson resonated with all our fans of the late Ray Harryhausen and it came as no surprise to us that quickly we had new scribes lining up to set sail with Sinbad and the crew of the Blue Nymph once again.

And here we are, within a year, launching our second voyage and our line-up of talent is stellar indeed. Kicking it off is another novella, this one by Ed Erdelac, one of my personal favorite writers in the New Pulp movement. Ed writes a series of weird westerns featuring a Hasidic Jewish Rabbi called the Merkabah Rider. Go out and find them; you'll be glad you did. Then we have two shorts, one by Airship 27 veteran, Erwin K. Roberts who has done several tales for us in various hero pulp anthologies. Lastly there is Shelby Vick, easily the oldest writer we've ever had the pleasure of publishing. Although a senior, there's nothing rusty about his writing talent or marvelous imagination as his swashbuckling yarn proves in this volume. We are thrilled to have him aboard.

In volume one Bryan Fowler provided a truly fantastic cover painting and Ralf van der Hoeven the gorgeous interior artwork; both being veteran creators with our label. For this volume we were extremely lucky to recruit two amazing new artists. Handling the interiors this time was Steven Wilcox who I came across on Facebook and was instantly taken by his drawing skills. He's done a bang up job with his Sinbad pieces. Also discovered via Facebook was Kevin Johnson, a retired army man who resides in Colorado Springs. Seeing several of Kevin's completed works on-line, I thought he'd be the perfect choice to capture our version of the famous seaman and he delivered a truly stunning painting.

So yes, Sinbad continues to voyage the high seas with his colorful crew and the future of this series seems brighter than ever. We are not only getting submissions for a volume three, but one ambitious writer has promised to deliver a full length novel to us soon. See what I mean? You just can't keep a classic hero like Sinbad at harbor for too long. The sea is his home, experiencing fantastic adventures his fate. We're just happy you all decided to come along.

Ron Fortier
7/18/2013
Fort Collins, CO.
(Airship27@comcast.net)
(www.Airship27.com)

Airship
27

A CLASSIC HERO REBORN

QUATERMAIN
THE NEW ADVENTURES
AARON SMITH • ALAN J. PORTER

British adventure writer, H. Rider Haggard's most popular fictional character was Alan Quatermain, the irascible African big game hunter. As the hero of the classic KING SOLOMON'S MINES, Quatermain immediately fired the imagination of readers across the world and created an instant demand for more of his adventures.

Now Airship 27 Productions answers that on-going demand by presenting two brand new Alan Quatermain novellas each filled with plenty of suspense, action and exotic African locales. When a French riverboat pilot discovers elephant ivory suffused with gold, it sends the expert guide on a quest to find a fabled elephant's graveyard to learn the answer to the "GOLDEN IVORY" by Alan J. Porter.

Next a naïve American lad follows Quatermain deep into the jungle to find eight missing white women only to uncover an ancient evil capable of possessing the bodies of its victim's in Aaron Smith's chilling "TEMPLE OF LOST SOULS."

Here are complete tales that will thrill pulp fans and introduce a whole new generation to one of the most famous adventure heroes of all time; H. Rider Haggard's Alan Quatermain.

AN AIRSHIP 27 PRODUCTION
AIRSHIP27HANGAR.COM
NEW PULP

PULP FICTION FOR A NEW GENERATION!

AVAILABLE AT AMAZON.COM AND
AIRSHIP27HANGAR.COM

VOLUME TWO COMING SOON!

RAVENWOOD
Stepson of Mystery

PULP FICTION FOR A NEW GENERATION!
FROM AMAZON.COM AND AIRSHIP27HANGAR.COM

AN AIRSHIP 27 PRODUCTION